"Please don't cry."

Jake lifted his finger to Brooke's cheek, brushing away a tear with paralyzing tenderness.

No, no, no! Brooke didn't want the drama and crying and that ridiculous have-to-have-you-or-I'll-die passion. She wanted…

Involuntarily, she looked at Jake, his profile as familiar and dear to her as if she'd known him her whole life, rather than just a month.

She closed her eyes and took a deep breath, when she opened them again, she found Jake meeting her gaze with disconcerting intimacy. He was far too close.

Heat flooded her body…and remorse flooded her mind.

"He's your best friend," she accused.

"And he deserves someone who really loves him. That's the one percent of me that's being noble. The other ninety-nine just wants to kiss you so bad I can't even think."

Dear Reader,

I admit it: I'm an incurable romantic. I'm a sucker for happy endings and I love weddings. Not just the big day but the exciting preparations beforehand that often bring together family and friends. Of course, some of that preparation can be just a tad stressful for the bride-to-be.

Especially if she secretly has doubts about the upcoming nuptials. And is finding the once-irritating best man more attractive by the moment.

Meet Brooke Nichols, the renegade sane person in the Nichols family. Growing up surrounded by unpredictable creative types, Brooke longed to one day build a calm, stable family of her own. Her engagement to handsome, successful Giff Baker seems like a dream come true! Yet no matter how much she insists that stability is far more important than illogical "chemistry," she sometimes wonders…

Brooke isn't the only one with doubts. Fireman Jake McBride has been Giff's best friend since childhood and is supposed to be the best man in the wedding. But he thinks this marriage will be a mistake—an opinion that does not endear him to the bride. Giff suggests that Brooke and Jake just need to spend more time together and get to know each other, but that leads to a whole new set of problems! Jake is forced to admit that Brooke is a wonderful woman. Unfortunately, he's starting to see her as a wonderful match for *him*. Brooke realizes that Jake is as loyal and warmhearted as he is gorgeous. But he's also a spontaneous free spirit—the complete opposite of the peaceful predictability she's craved her whole life.

The road to a happy ending may not be smooth, but I hope you'll enjoy the journey, bumps and all!

Tanya Michaels

The Best Man in Texas
TANYA MICHAELS

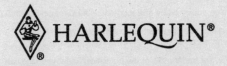

TORONTO • NEW YORK • LONDON
AMSTERDAM • PARIS • SYDNEY • HAMBURG
STOCKHOLM • ATHENS • TOKYO • MILAN • MADRID
PRAGUE • WARSAW • BUDAPEST • AUCKLAND

Recycling programs
for this product may
not exist in your area.

ISBN-13: 978-0-373-75315-4

THE BEST MAN IN TEXAS

Copyright © 2010 by Tanya Michna.

This edition published by arrangement with Harlequin Books S.A.

For questions and comments about the quality of this book
please contact us at Customer_eCare@Harlequin.ca

® and TM are trademarks of the publisher. Trademarks indicated with
® are registered in the United States Patent and Trademark Office, the
Canadian Trade Marks Office and in other countries.

www.eHarlequin.com

Printed in U.S.A.

ABOUT THE AUTHOR

Tanya Michaels began telling stories almost as soon as she could talk...and started stealing her mom's Harlequin romances less than a decade later. In 2003, Tanya was thrilled to have her first book, a romantic comedy, published by Harlequin Books. Since then, Tanya has sold more than twenty books and is a two-time recipient of a Booksellers' Best Award as well as a finalist for the Holt Medallion, National Readers' Choice Award and Romance Writers of America's prestigious RITA® Award. Tanya lives in Georgia with her husband, two children and an unpredictable cat, but you can visit Tanya online at www.tanyamichaels.com.

Books by Tanya Michaels

HARLEQUIN AMERICAN ROMANCE

1170—TROUBLE IN TENNESSEE
1203—AN UNLIKELY MOMMY
1225—A DAD FOR HER TWINS
1235—MISTLETOE BABY*
1255—MISTLETOE CINDERELLA*
1270—MISTLETOE MOMMY*
1279—MISTLETOE HERO*

HARLEQUIN TEMPTATION

968—HERS FOR THE WEEKEND
986—SHEER DECADENCE
1008—GOING ALL THE WAY

*4 Seasons in Mistletoe

This story is a Texas-based celebration
of love and family, so it is fittingly dedicated
to newlyweds Lara Spiker Williams (congrats, sis!)
and Marc Williams (welcome to the family).

Chapter One

Brooke Nichols had grown up in a family where random announcements and dramatic proclamations were a way of life.

Girls, your mother has kicked me out of the house... again.

How would you two like to blow off school today and drive to SeaWorld?

Mom, Dad, Brooke, check it out! I decided to shave my head.

In contrast to her parents' and older sister, Meg's, more colorful news, Brooke had always announced academic success, such as the journalism scholarship to the University of Texas, or updates about her job, which was currently writing for the Community Lifestyles section of the *Katy Chronicle*. None of her declarations had ever caught anyone off guard. But tonight Brooke had something to share that was both life changing and unexpected.

At least, I didn't see it coming, Brooke mused as she approached the front door of her parents' most recent rental home. She'd barely set foot on the porch when her mom emerged from the house, the screen door clattering behind her.

"There's the birthday girl!" Didi Nichols enthused. The slim woman with her long, wheat-blond hair was barefoot beneath a baby-doll dress, her only makeup a bright pink smear of lip gloss. When people saw Didi out with Meg, they assumed mother and daughter were sisters. When they saw Didi with curvier, dark-haired Brooke, they didn't suspect any relation at all. "Come in, come in. Get out of this heat."

Although it was only mid-May, with months of summer still ahead, temperatures in south Texas had been climbing all week. Inside the house, the air conditioner hummed through the ceiling vents, causing a lavender-and-yellow Happy Birthday banner to flutter overhead. Brooke half chuckled at the whimsical acknowledgment of her thirtieth year.

Following her daughter's gaze upward, Didi grinned. "You know me, I never throw anything away. That old thing probably dates back to one of Meg's preteen surprise parties."

While Brooke used to make her parents swear they wouldn't ambush her with a party—she'd found adolescent social occasions awkward enough when she *was* prepared—Meg loved the unexpected and dropped heavy hints every year that she would welcome another surprise party. Which, ironically, led to them never being much of a surprise.

"Your sister was so sorry she couldn't make it," Didi said. "With that course she's taking during the day, she's back to waitressing nights, and Saturdays are big business."

After trying and rejecting cosmetology classes and an apprenticeship to a dessert chef, Meg was now training to be a private investigator.

Brooke nodded. "Giff wishes he could be here, too, but he flew to San Francisco first thing this morning." She caught herself absently fidgeting with the flawless diamond-solitaire ring. Even though she and Gifford Baker had never discussed engagement before last night, much less window-shopped for jewelry, he'd managed to find a ring that fit perfectly—which was so like him.

Didi pursed her lips. "Maybe it would have been better if we'd scheduled this for another time instead of on your actual birthday. Not much of a celebration with just me and Dad, is it? Do you remember that blowout we had for my fiftieth?"

"Yeah, that was…pretty unforgettable." Brooke managed not to wince at the memory of crowded chaos. When the police had shown up with a noise complaint, one of Didi's "free-spirited" friends had flashed him in an attempt to earn his goodwill. "Trust me, I'm fine with just the three of us. I have something I want to tell you and Dad anyway."

Didi's dark eyes widened with concern. She obviously hadn't noticed the engagement ring. "That sounds serious, dear."

Very. Rest-of-her-life serious.

Brooke had spent years carefully laying out what she wanted her future to be like, what kind of family she would build. Her own children would enjoy a comforting, *stable* life. Giff—intelligent, reliable and, as a bonus, movie star handsome—could give her everything she'd ever wanted.

She felt a smile tug at her lips as she envisioned her long-cherished dreams coming true. "Don't worry, Mom, it's—"

But her mother was moving toward the kitchen. "Everett? Come in here, honey! Brooke has something she needs to discuss with us."

A moment later Everett Nichols loped into the room, his long-legged stride unhampered by the apron he wore. He passed by his wife to squash his daughter in a bear hug. "Hope you're hungry, baby. I'm trying something new in honor of your birthday."

Brooke's parents had met in Vegas, where Didi had dealt blackjack and Everett had been trying to work his way up in a resort kitchen despite his lack of formal training. A potentially brilliant chef plagued by moments of outrageous failure, he refused to play it safe with flavors. When his criticism of the head chef's "predictable palate" cost him his job, Everett had gone to a nearby casino to drown his sorrows. According to family legend, his gaze had locked with Didi's and they were married within seventy-two hours.

In high school and college, Brooke's friends had giggled over the "passion" of it, how romantic it was that her parents had shared such a whirlwind courtship. Of course, none of her friends had lived through her parents' subsequent marriage, marked as it was with its *passionate* arguments. And reconciliations. And spontaneous decisions like sinking all the money into a family restaurant that hadn't lasted three months, or abruptly moving the family to Colorado while Brooke was in elementary school and then to Texas in the middle of her eighth-grade year.

Brooke's shoulders straightened as if a burden had been lifted. When Giff had asked her last night to be his wife, she'd experienced a twinge—a whisper, really—of doubt. They'd been dating exclusively since the night, not that long ago, they'd been introduced at a charity St. Patrick's Day gala. And while she appreciated his brilliance as a technologies consultant, his work ethic and his devotion to his mother, who was recovering from breast cancer, Brooke had occasionally taken stock of her feelings and wondered if there should be…more. Now, looking at her two impetuous parents and thinking about how different her own marriage with Giff would be, Brooke knew without a doubt she'd been right to accept his proposal.

In our case, maybe less really is more.

Prompted by the way his wife was nervously twisting her hands, Everett asked, "Brooke, is everything all right?"

"Couldn't be better." She beamed at them and held out her left hand. "Mom, Dad, I'm getting married!"

Chapter Two

From the passenger seat came a sudden chirp. Someone must have left a voice mail earlier. Steering one-handed, Jake McBride kept his eyes on the freeway while digging through maps, CD cases and the balled-up paper bag that had held his lunch a few hours ago. His stomach rumbled. *All right, more than a few.*

Finally he retrieved the phone. He'd spent a good part of the day driving through the boonies, where reception was questionable, so it was unsurprising that he'd missed a call. Without glancing at the small glowing screen—how many accidents had he seen on the job caused by people looking at their phones or scrolling through iPod menus?—he held the cell to his ear and fumbled with buttons until a computerized female voice told him he had two new messages.

"Hoskins here," began the first recording. The most recent addition at the fire station, Ben Hoskins didn't have much experience yet, but he was a quick learner and an affable guy. "Don't know how late you'll roll in, but we're looking at an urgent Bravo Echo Echo Romeo down at Buck's tonight. Could use your expertise."

Jake shook his head, chuckling under his breath at the rookie's invitation to join the guys for a beer. More enticing than the prospect of a drink was the fact that Buck's had the best jalapeño burger in the state. Still, after four days out of town, Jake needed to shower, unpack and catch a night's sleep in his own bed, so maybe he'd pass on Buck's.

After years in the army, the concept of having his own bed and a permanent address to go with it was still rather new. Following his return to the States and honorable discharge, Jake had bought a place on the rural outskirts of Katy, about half an hour from where he'd grown up in Houston. His small, unassuming house was comfortable enough, but coming back from these trips and walking through the front door never gave him that emotional "aha!" moment. There was no soothing rush of *home* other guys in his Company had often reminisced about.

One could argue that Jake's stint in the military, the string of temporary assignments and lodgings, had contributed to his footloose tendency, but the truth was, he'd always been restless. He had endless childhood memories of his mother imploring him to "settle down," "sit down" or "quiet down." Especially if Jake's father had been sleeping off his latest overindulgence.

Pushing aside the recollection of his parents, Jake pressed a button and listened to the second phone message.

"Hey." Giff's voice, as familiar as a brother's, provoked a stab of guilt. How long had it been since they'd met for a game of racquetball or a platter of burritos at

Jake's favorite Mexican restaurant, Comida Buena? "I know you were away on one of your walkabouts this weekend."

Jake grinned at his friend's phrasing.

"I'm actually on the West Coast myself, lending a hand with a product rollout, but I get back on Wednesday. You free for dinner that night? I have news that I want to give in person. Nothing bad," Giff added hastily. With a self-conscious laugh, he said, "Just the opposite. I've got to run, but give me a call tomorrow if you get a chance."

Intrigued, Jake tossed the cell phone back onto the passenger seat. He appreciated the assurance that everything was okay since Jake's first thought had been of Grace Baker. Giff's mom had fought a rocky battle with breast cancer during Jake's last tour. If his friend had something to celebrate, it could help restore Jake's faith in the universe. He'd seen tragic things happen to decent people, *young* people.

As a kid, the son of a disabled and bitter former policeman who increasingly prioritized booze over his wife and child, Jake had fatalistically accepted that *his* life sucked, but he'd believed in some sort of cosmic balance. Surely people born into better neighborhoods and sober families had no worries. Then one spring day in fourth grade, he'd encountered Gifford Baker—the only child of wealthy, loving parents—who was about to get his ass kicked in the field behind the school. By the time they were sophomores, Giff was six feet and spent every morning in the weight room. But such was not the case in fourth grade when three bullies had cornered him. He'd already taken one blow to the face when Jake crested the hill.

Jake hadn't known Giff, only known of him. Every class had been required to write a thank-you note to Mr. Baker's corporation for the money donated to air-condition the gymnasium. It wasn't affection that propelled Jake to the other boy's defense, but an overwhelming sense of *wrongness*. If even people like Gifford Baker had crappy stuff happen to them, what hope was there for anyone else?

In the weeks following Jake's impromptu rescue, the boys became best friends. On their high school football team, Jake played fullback to Giff's running back, blocking and protecting as necessary. They'd roomed together for a year at Texas A&M until Giff took a semester off when his father died. Jake had never been brave enough to ask, but he couldn't help wondering if Giff ever resented that it had been *his* father—a philanthropist who'd adored his family—instead of, say, an embittered alcoholic whose wife cried nightly and whose son spent as little time home as possible.

Nothing bad, Giff had promised this time. *Just the opposite.*

Something good, then. Even without knowing what it was, Jake was happy for his friend already. He looked forward to getting the details in a couple of days. Who deserved "good" more than Gifford Baker?

"Okay, now that *she's* gone…" Megan Nichols began conspiratorially.

Brooke blinked. "Who? Kresley?" Her friend and

editor, Kresley Flynn, had just excused herself to the ladies' room—which she'd been doing more frequently as her pregnancy progressed.

"Yeah." Meg scooted closer, temporarily taking Kresley's chair so that Brooke could better hear her over the rockabilly band playing in the next room. Buck's Bar and Grill was foremost a restaurant, but a side room off of the main dining area offered darts, pool and a dance floor not much bigger than a cracker. "I didn't want to say anything in front of her that sounded unsupportive— I mean, family solidarity here—but I have to ask, are you sure about this? The engagement?"

"Am I sure?" Brooke echoed, nonplussed. Her big sister's motto was to leap first and look…eventually. If she got around to feeling like it. Meg was the *last* person Brooke would have expected to question her decision. Maybe getting engaged after just two months of dating would seem quick to some, but two months was practically a decade in Nichols years. "Why wouldn't I be?"

"Well." Meg smiled hesitantly, the expression in her big brown eyes pitying. "I admit Giff is a great-looking guy. That's undeniable. But his being easy on the eyes aside, don't you sometimes find him a bit dull?"

An undignified bark of laughter escaped Brooke. So that was Megan's big concern? "Meg, the last guy you went out with for more than a week swallowed swords and juggled fire at the Texas Renaissance Festival. Compared to that, anyone's bound to seem dull. Giff isn't boring, he's dependable."

Meg wrinkled her nose, looking closer to twenty than thirty-five. "Another word for predictable."

If I'm lucky. Despite herself, Brooke had once fallen for a guy outside her comfort zone—a fellow writer she'd met during her college years in Austin. Her tumultuous on-again, off-again year with the gorgeous brooding poet had reinforced her belief that she didn't need any more spontaneous types or "artistic temperaments" in her life. Now she had a gorgeous businessman who always called when he said he would and would never forget her birthday. Nothing could make her happier.

"Don't confuse me with you," Brooke said gently. "I'm the one who *doesn't* like surprises."

With a sigh, Meg flipped her blond hair over her shoulder. "All right. But at least tell me that you two celebrated with a night of wild—"

"What did I miss?" Kresley asked, returning to the table and waiting patiently for Meg to slide back to her own chair. Kresley was adorable in a tie-dyed maternity top, and her thick blond hair was shampoo-ad shiny; she credited the pre-natal vitamins.

Once her coworker was seated again, Brooke felt like the token brunette at the table.

"Just in time," Meg said, her voice full of mischief. "I was about to get the down and dirty details of Brooke's sex life. I mean, now that you're engaged, you *did* finally—"

"Meg, he's going to be the father of my kids. Your brother-in-law. This isn't some sordid one-night stand."

"Don't knock it till you've tried it," Meg teased. She

herself was not shy about details. In her early twenties, she'd traumatized her sister with explicit firsthand descriptions of what sexual positions offered the best orgasms. It had taken sixteen-year-old Brooke a week to get the unwanted images out of her head.

Brooke resisted the urge to point out that rushing into bed had never gained Meg anything lasting and meaningful. *Not my place to judge.* After all, Meg had never craved something permanent the way Brooke did.

But passion wasn't everything. Brooke had shared incredible physical chemistry with her long-ago poet, and that relationship had been a fiasco. By the time they'd broken up for good, she'd been such a mess that she'd almost lost her university scholarship.

Apparently not even Kresley understood Brooke's inclination to take it slow, to prioritize the emotional bond over sex. Her pale eyebrows were arched in disbelief. "So does that mean you guys still haven't—"

"Not that it's any of your business," Brooke pointed out, "but we decided it would be romantic to wait until our wedding night."

Meg snorted. "At least now I understand the rush to get married this summer."

When Giff got back from California this week, they were going to look into different venues and date availability. But they agreed that late July or early August suited them both. He was already scheduled to travel during much of September and, as he'd reasoned, now that they'd found the person they each wanted to spend forever with, why delay? Besides, they wanted at least a year alone together before they started building a family. The risk of pregnancy complications went up significantly after thirty-five, and not everyone was lucky enough to conceive as quickly as Kresley and her husband, Dane.

Brooke shot a wistful glance in Kresley's direction. The lifestyles editor was one of those blue-eyed, blond, former cheerleaders who'd been beautiful all her life, but in Brooke's opinion the woman had never looked lovelier than she did now that she was expecting. Of course, Brooke might be biased because she herself had always wanted to be a mom. Every time she'd felt shocked or embarrassed as an adolescent, she'd resolved to do things differently with her own kids. Those imaginary kids had gradually taken shape in her vivid imagination. She wanted to be ridiculously domestic, cooking them spaghetti and meat loaf instead of asking them to try wasabi brownies; she wanted to help them with her homework and sew silly costumes for school plays.

Granted, she'd never actually made a meat loaf and didn't own a sewing machine. But these were minor technicalities.

Kresley interrupted Brooke's fond plans for her future family. "I for one am relieved that you're looking at July for the wedding. It's bad enough that I'm going to be a pregnant bridesmaid, but by September, someone would have to *roll* me to the front of the church."

Brooke laughed. "You're not that big. Besides, you should be happy you've gained weight."

For the first trimester, Kresley had been sick as a dog. Unable to hold down foods or liquids—hell, she'd barely been able to hold down *air*—she'd lost a few pounds.

"It is nice to have my appetite back," Kresley admitted with a sheepish look at Brooke's empty plate. After Kresley had demolished her own salad, she'd finished Brooke's nachos.

"Speaking of food—" Meg rose "—I should do a once-around, make sure no one's in the weeds."

When the three women had first agreed to celebrate Brooke's news and discuss wedding plans over dinner, Megan hadn't been scheduled to work on Monday. But another waitress had called in sick, and Buck himself had promised them free food if Meg would be on the premises as "just in case" backup. Brooke had to admit her sister was a popular waitress; even with the minimal amount of work she'd done tonight, she'd made good tips. Meg's last waitressing job had been at a four-star restaurant but required skirts and pantyhose. Meg had ditched that in favor of wearing blue jeans and a black T-shirt to work.

Once Meg had left to make her rounds, Kresley flashed an evil grin. "Brave move of you, asking your sister to be your maid of honor. You're not worried about bizarre ceremony surprises or a bachelorette party that gets so out of hand the police are called?"

Valid concerns. In theory, the sooner they had the wedding, the less time Meg would have to plan something outrageous. But the truth was, Meg wasn't much of a planner. She'd never had a problem manufacturing last-minute outrageousness.

"She's my sister," Brooke said by way of resigned explanation. "I couldn't *not* ask her. Especially since you're in your second trimester and—"

"I was only giving you a hard time," Kresley assured her. "I'm not hurt that you didn't ask me."

"Promise me that if she tries to draft you for something insane, you'll remind her that I don't like surprises?"

Kresley's eyes twinkled. "If you think that'll do any good."

Brooke traced the rim of her glass. "Do you think it's rushing to get married in just a few months?"

"Not if you keep it simple. You said you both wanted a small, intimate wedding, right? Rushing would be if you two crazy kids had up and eloped."

"No. That is emphatically not for me." Her stomach clenched at the thought. For someone who wanted a marriage so different from her parents', kicking off the marriage in the exact same way seemed like a bad omen. "Besides it would break Grace's heart if she wasn't there."

Giff had told her he'd shown his mom the ring before he'd taken Brooke to dinner last Friday; they'd gone to see her afterward to share the happy news. The woman was as warm and caring as her son, and Brooke knew she'd make a wonderful mother-in-law.

"We're having Sunday supper with her this weekend," Brooke said. "Giff offered to take us all out somewhere, but she said she has to cook to properly welcome me into the family." Grace probably knew a great meat loaf recipe.

"She's his only family?" Kresley asked.

"Pretty much. He has an uncle in Dallas, some cousins he's not really close to that I'll meet eventually. But next to his mom, the most important person to him is a guy he grew up with. They were apparently like brothers—I'm supposed to meet him Wednesday. If Giff loves him, I'm sure I will, too."

"Whoa." They heard Meg's return before they saw her. She launched herself back into her chair, fanning herself dramatically with what looked like a magazine. "You guys should really go play pool."

"Um, I tire pretty easily these days," Kresley admitted. "I was considering going home to bed."

"But you're missing out!" Meg dropped what she was holding on the table, and Brooke realized it was actually a calendar. "There are three seriously hunky firemen in the next room. I refilled a drink for one, and we got to talking about these calendars they did as a community fundraiser. He gave me this one at a discount since the year's half over."

Brooke laughed. "I don't think I've ever seen a calendar at your apartment." Meg's only concession to structured time management were a few clocks, but the one in her living room had been stopped for months. Brooke always wanted to sneak in with batteries and reset it.

"Trust me, sis, this calendar I *will* be hanging up." She began flipping through it so they could all see the pictures.

January's photo featured a man with a great smile who was leaning across an old-fashioned fire engine, his hand on the gold bell. The caption read Ringing in the New Year. Overall, it was a politically correct calendar that no one would be embarrassed to have in their kitchen. A couple of female firefighters were included, and no one was posed in a bright red thong. But the men who'd been chosen for the summer months were all shirtless, and Brooke's breath caught when she noticed Mr. July.

The man on the page had chiseled cheekbones and a jawline dusted with dark stubble. His light brown hair was cropped close, extremely short on the sides but long enough to be tousled on top. His arms were amazingly well defined without making him look like a professional weight lifter. It was his eyes that captivated her, though. She wasn't sure if it was their unusual clear green color or something in his gaze that—

Meg snapped the calendar closed. "A few of these guys are actually in the next room! Come on, we can go ogle the life-size versions."

Brooke cleared her throat, self-conscious over just how intently she'd been ogling already. Was *he* one of the three men in the billiards room? She squelched her flare of curiosity, calling Giff's face to mind. "No thanks. You forget, Kres and I are both in happy, monogamous relationships. *And* we both have to be at the office for a staff meeting at seven-thirty tomorrow morning."

"She's right," Kresley seconded. But that didn't stop her from casting a wistful glance in the direction Meg had indicated. "I need to get going."

Pressing a hand to her forehead, Meg mumbled, "I can't believe I'm related to someone who would voluntarily pass up this opportunity. Are you sure you weren't adopted?"

"You tell me," Brooke said with a laugh. "You were

there first." Being adopted would certainly explain why she usually felt like an outsider among her own family.

But that would all change soon. Once she and Giff were married, they'd build the life she'd always wanted.

Chapter Three

It occurred to Jake Wednesday evening as he walked through the stone archway and inhaled the smell of peppers and grilled meats that this was as close as he'd ever come to that elusive *home* sentiment. Though it might be no more than a hole-in-the-wall, to Jake the family-owned Comida Buena was heaven. Assuming angels ate garlicky guacamole.

Giff was already inside, waiting for his turn at the hostess podium. His face broke into a wide smile when he spotted Jake. "McBride!" They leaned forward, each slugging an arm around the other man's shoulders. If people were surprised to see two former football players who topped six feet hugging, well…Jake didn't give a rat's ass.

"Glad you could make it," Giff said.

"My pleasure." Jake pointed at the uniform he wore. "But I'm on call, so no cerveza for me. I promised to bring back tamales for the guys at the station."

They followed the hostess past a large black velvet painting of a rooster and brightly decorated sombreros hanging on the wall to a booth in the back. A busboy moving with superhero-like stealth tossed a basket of chips onto the table, then disappeared as quickly as he'd arrived; Jake knew from experience not to touch the fiery house salsa until glasses of water had been poured.

Once they'd been given their drinks and had placed their orders, Jake got straight to the point. "So, Mr. Mystery, what's the big news?"

Giff leaned back against the padded bench, managing to look at home in the shabby interior despite his dress shirt and slacks—a designer suit minus matching blazer and tie—probably costing close to what Jake had paid for his first car. At least, what he'd paid to *own* the hunk of junk. He'd poured a ton of money into rebuilding it.

Responding to Jake's bluntness with his own, Giff announced without preamble, "I'm engaged."

Engaged?

Engaged to be married?

Jake had been peripherally aware that Giff had a girlfriend. He had not known it was so serious. "That does qualify as good," he said distractedly, trying to process the news.

"I certainly think so," Giff drawled.

"What…when?"

"I proposed to her last Friday, before I left town. And we'd like to be married by late summer."

Her. Some faceless stranger was about to become Giff's future. Surreal. "Her name's…" Jake searched his memory. *River? Lake?* "Brooke, right?"

Giff nodded. "Brooke Nichols."

"And you've been dating since…?"

"We met on St. Patrick's Day. It's been about two months."

Jake couldn't prevent a wry chuckle. Even back in the fourth grade, faced by jealous punks from less privileged families, Giff had seemed oblivious of his own wealth. He was generous and unpretentious, but the fact remained some men would have needed to save up for the ring for longer than Giff had actually *known* his fiancée.

"Two months, huh? That's—" *Unlike you.* "Bold."

Companies around the country hired Giff to consult because of his analytical mind. He liked to study a problem from every possible angle before he recommended a course of action. This Brooke must be quite a girl for him to move so fast.

"I think I was channeling you," Giff confided with a grin.

In what universe could anyone associate Jake with betrothal? The most stable, permanent thing in his whole life had been his friendship with Giff. Although Jake didn't think of himself as commitment-phobic—definitely not one of those pitiful fools trying to pick up a different woman every weekend—he hadn't sustained many relationships, either. He couldn't picture himself married.

He couldn't even picture himself proposing.

"I'm not sure I get the comparison," Jake admitted. "I've never been close to asking someone to marry me."

"No, but you're fearless. You don't hesitate to rush in

headlong. You've often told me 'life is short.' And this thing with Mom being sick..." Giff glanced away.

"She's better now, though?" Jake's flare of anxiety belied the "fearless" label. Grace Baker had been a second mother to him, loving him wholeheartedly. Since his return to Texas, he'd made more of a point to visit her than his own family. Although his mom had assured him that his father had quit drinking, for good this time.

"She insists she's fine." Giff shook his head as if to physically dislodge his own worry. "She even fussed at me last month when I asked how she was. She told me to stop driving her crazy with concern and go live my own life. That's what I'm doing. With Brooke."

Vague uneasiness rippled through Jake. In both the military and in his service as a firefighter/paramedic, he'd seen people cope with life-and-death situations. Sometimes coming face to face with your mortality or that of a loved one led to knee-jerk reactions. Giff had no siblings, had lost his father and had lived under the threat of losing his mother. Was he so worried about losing his family that he was trying to throw a new one together? An understandable motivation, but one that might not lead to a smooth future and the happiness Giff deserved.

Jake hesitated to voice that thought. Instead, he said cautiously, "So tell me about Brooke."

"She's terrific—smart, gorgeous, supportive. Her only possible flaw is being a Longhorn," Giff joked. A&M's Aggies had a long-standing rivalry with the University of Texas. "But I've decided to forgive her that. She's going to be a fantastic mother. She works at a newspaper for now. I think she wants to stay home after the kids are born, at least for their early years."

The kids? Once again Jake found himself disoriented. How had they zoomed straight from popping the question to parenthood? It seemed so rash, so uncharacteristic of Giff, that Jake couldn't help wondering if Brooke had been pushing the idea. Was she one of those women whose biological clock was ticking like a time bomb?

The cynical part of him couldn't help thinking that if they had kids right away, she'd be able to quit work even sooner. Was she swayed by Giff's wealth and the idea of a more leisurely lifestyle?

"The two of you have a lot in common?" Jake prodded. "Does her family hail from River Oaks, too?"

Giff laughed at his friend's exaggeration in mentioning one of Houston's most affluent communities. "*I* couldn't even afford a place in River Oaks. But, no, she doesn't come from money. You of all people know that's not important to me."

For a moment Jake was ashamed of himself for even asking. "Yeah, I know." But just because it was unimportant to Giff didn't mean it was equally inconsequential to a prospective bride.

Suddenly Giff's gaze went past Jake, and the man smiled. "Surprise. Here's your chance to find out about Brooke for yourself instead of just listening to me babble." He stood, signaling.

Following suit, Jake rose and looked behind him, curiously scanning the restaurant. He only had an impression of a dark-haired woman wearing yellow. His view was blocked by a waiter who carried a tray of fajitas that were still audibly sizzling.

And then she came into sight. Giff had said she'd make a fantastic mother, but maternal wasn't the first thing that sprang to Jake's mind when he saw her. She was sleek and lush all at once, wearing a canary-yellow silk blouse and black pencil skirt. The clothes accentuated a great figure but were way overdressed for Comida Buena, like the tuxedoed teenagers one saw in pancake houses after prom. Her brown hair, nearly black, was cut in a bob, the jagged layering around her face lending her edge. And her eyes—

Had just gone as wide as two tortillas.

She stopped cold as she reached Jake, her voice so low that he barely heard her words. "Oh, my God. You're Mr. July."

Chapter Four

"F-from the calendar," the brunette babbled, making a wider circle than necessary to sidestep him. She tilted her face upward to absently accept Giff's kiss on the cheek, but her startled gaze remained on Jake. "My sister has a calendar, and you— The fire department…"

"Ah." Jake realized now what she was talking about. He glanced across the table to Giff, who looked puzzled. "That fundraiser I told you about at Christmas?"

"My sister, Meg, bought one of them," Brooke interjected. "I just wasn't expecting Mr. July to be the best man at my…" Trailing off, she shot Giff an apologetic glance. "Did you have a chance to ask him yet?"

"We were working our way to that," he said.

"Oh." She shoved a hand through her hair, somehow without messing it up; every strand slid neatly back into place. Then she turned to face Jake again. "We're still hammering out the specifics, but we plan to have the wedding soon."

"That's what I hear." Now that he'd seen the bride-to-be, he was even more surprised at the seeming urgency. Impeccably put together, she looked like one of those women who wanted things *just so,* the kind who would actually enjoy fussing over little details such as seating charts and color-coordinating ribbons with flowers.

"Once Giff and I settle on a date, we'll let you know ASAP so you can put it on your—" Her cheeks flushed with color.

"Calendar?" Jake supplied with a grin. Was it pre-nuptial nerves, or did she always fluster this easily? His photo had been a pretty tame picture for a good cause, nothing that warranted blushing. Or, for that matter, memorizing. If she hadn't been his best friend's fiancée, Jake might have found it flattering that she'd known exactly who he was when July was still two months away.

She was covering her moment of embarrassment with newly squared shoulders and a brisk tone. "Hopefully there won't be any schedule conflicts for you."

Before Jake could tell her that nothing would get in the way of his standing up for the man who'd been like a brother to him, Giff chuckled. "I doubt we have to worry about that. Jake likes to keep his schedule wide open, be spontaneous."

That was true. After years of rigid structure in the Army and, to a lesser degree, the protocol at the fire station, he now used his personal time to experiment with a different way of life. "I like to be free to go wherever the mood takes me."

"You would get along great with my sister." Brooke's expression was neutral, but there was a flat undertone in her voice that made Jake wonder if *she* got along with her sister.

Giff hit his palm to his forehead. "I haven't even properly introduced the two of you. Brooke, meet Jake McBride. Jake, Brooke Nichols."

Jake reached across the table to shake her hand, which she pulled back the instant good manners allowed. Not exactly a warm, gushing bride-to-be. Shouldn't she be glowing with happiness and proudly displaying the engagement ring or something?

She turned to Giff. "I'm going to run to the ladies' room. Will you order for me if the waitress comes back before I do?"

"Sure. You want your usual?" Giff asked.

"Absolutely. The number three, as always." She gave Jake a tight smile. "Not all of us were born with the spontaneity gene."

He watched her go, trying to form a first impression. Was her parting shot a jab at him, or an attempt at self-deprecating humor? There was a…starchiness about her that made it easy to believe she wasn't the spontaneous type. And having seen her briefly with Giff, a man known for his thoughtful analysis of situations, Jake couldn't say that either of them looked swept away with passion for each other.

So why the rush to get married?

WELL. BROOKE MET HER EYES in the ladies' room mirror. *That could have gone better.*

She sighed. Some people, especially Meg, never quite believed her when she insisted she disliked surprises, but tonight was proving her point. When confronted with the

unexpected—such as green-eyed Mr. July—she tended
to stiffen up as though bracing for impact.

Her life had been peppered with strange announcements and incoming decisions that she'd had no control
over. Instead of growing more accustomed to them over
time, they'd made her almost brittle. As if the next thing
that startled her might send her over the edge. Taking
a deep breath, Brooke reassured herself that life with
Giff would hold blessedly few surprises.

He planned ahead and always did as promised. *Exactly* what she needed. Of course, right now, the guy of
her dreams was probably sitting out in the dining room
trying to explain to his best friend why she'd behaved so
awkwardly. Giff had made it clear that, next to Grace,
Jake McBride was the most important person in his
life. Which meant that Jake would be important in *their*
life.

Damage control time, she decided as she reached
for the door. She would go back to the table and make
friends with Mr. McBride. She would not be thrown off
by the fact that his face—and bare chest—happened
to be featured on some calendar of Meg's. Or that
he was, impossibly, better-looking in person than in
photograph.

Knock it off. So the guy was attractive. Big whoop.
Brooke was engaged to one of the best-looking men in
the entire Houston metropolitan area, so there was no
reason for her to experience this flutter of...of— Whatever it was, she planned to ignore it.

Newly resolved, she exited the restroom and wound
her way back through tables that were starting to fill up

with diners as the hour grew later. She had to stop several times in the wake of servers who balanced steaming plates halfway up their arms.

Standing semi-camouflaged behind one such waiter not far from Giff's booth, she was in position to overhear his friend.

"…just saying, what's the hurry? Don't you want time to think it over so you don't make a mistake?"

"You realize that you're implying Brooke is a mistake?" Giff pointed out, sounding more exasperated than outraged on her behalf.

"Maybe she is," Jake pressed. "I—"

The waiter moved away, leaving Brooke exposed. Her horrified gaze met her fiancé's, and his expression was enough to stop McBride in midsentence.

Oh, hell. She ground her teeth through an unpleasant rush of déjà vu, every moment she'd ever had where she wished the earth would just swallow her whole. Mercifully her humiliation morphed quickly into anger. What did *she* have to be embarrassed about? Jake was the one who'd been making rude remarks; not even Meg was so uncouth that she'd challenge the engagement while Giff was on the actual premises.

Still, Brooke couldn't let Jake infuriate her into equal rudeness, not if she was going to befriend him. She refused to start her marriage to Giff feeling like she didn't belong in his inner circle. Like she didn't fit in. *Again.* She plastered a smile as bright as the Vegas Strip across her face. What was that old proverb, something about killing people with kindness?

Giff was already on his feet. "Brooke. I know you must have overheard—"

"Overheard a lifelong friend expressing concern for your well-being?" she interrupted.

"Thank you." Jake's tone was gruff. "I'm glad you realize that, under the circumstances, my question was perfectly normal and nothing against you personally."

Inwardly she rolled her eyes. Of course it was against her personally, as she was the only woman in the world engaged to Giff. With effort, she kept her voice so honey-sweet that the kitchen staff could have drizzled it over the sopaipillas. "I'm sure we'll look back on this moment and laugh."

Giff nodded gratefully. "Say, on our fiftieth wedding anniversary, when we've shown Jake how needless his worrying was."

"I look forward to it." Jake raised his glass in their direction, but there was still an assessing glint in his eyes that made Brooke feel as if she weren't being toasted. She was being challenged.

"So, APPARENTLY GIFF'S best friend is the devil." Brooke made this announcement from one of the chairs on the other side of Kresley's desk.

Since the two of them tended to show up in the small newspaper office earlier than most of their coworkers, it had become their ritual to take turns bringing in breakfast and chatting for a few minutes before officially starting their days. Kresley used to favor strong coffee and pastries she would later work off at her gym. Currently she preferred low-acid orange juice and granola bars. Brooke had felt almost guilty ordering her own cheese danish. *Maybe I should consider those granola bars, too.* She planned to spend Saturday trying on wedding dresses. The last thing she wanted was to go up a size.

Kresley arched a blond brow. "Dinner last night didn't go well? Giff's such a teddy bear that I imagined any buddy of his was a sweetheart, too."

Sweetheart? Was there a *less* accurate word to describe the intense and skeptical Jake McBride? "I don't think McBride approves of the engagement. But he told me not to take it personally," Brooke added.

"He actually had the gall to say he didn't approve? Of *you?*" Kresley's indignation was comforting. "Who the hell does this guy think he is?"

"Funny you should ask. You remember that calendar Meg showed us Monday night? The firemen?" When her friend nodded, Brooke said, "Giff's best friend, Jake, is Mr. July."

Kresley bit her bottom lip, looking thoughtful. "Which one was he? I remember all the summer months featured shirtless hotties, but nothing more specific than that. Blame pregnancy brain. I barely remember what street I live on."

"Jake's got brown hair, cut pretty short. He's…" As she tried to think how to describe him, Brooke squirmed in her seat. She opted for glib exaggeration. "Cheekbones that could cut glass, eyes that could tempt a woman to sell her soul. You know the type," she concluded with a nonchalant shrug.

"One of those good-looking but cocky guys? I hate him already."

"I wouldn't say that, exactly. Yes, he is good-looking. And there was definitely evidence of a little arrogance. But he's not a completely self-absorbed egomaniac. It's clear he feels protective of Giff."

"Protective?" Kresley made a dismissive sound. "Giff's over six feet tall and a wealthy man. He can take care of himself."

Brooke found herself wondering if the wealth was an issue for Jake; the only time he'd been prickly with Giff was when the check had arrived and the two macho men had argued over who got to pick up the tab.

"Hell, no, I won't let you pay," Jake had said. "This is a celebration. Consider dinner a gift to you and the lucky lady."

Giff had given up then, smiling down at Brooke. "*I'm* the lucky one."

Pulling herself back to the present, Brooke straightened in her seat. "Am I bringing enough to this marriage?"

"What?" Kresley looked confused.

"Me and Giff. As you pointed out, he does have money. And looks. And a heart the size of Texas."

Kresley set her cup down so hard that orange juice probably would have sloshed out were it not for the plastic lid. "Do *not* tell me this July jerk is making you question whether you're good enough for Giff."

"Not exactly. I just…"

It wasn't like Brooke to dwell on the past, especially with such a bright future to look forward to, but she recalled the intense emotional highs she'd experienced when she was twenty. Her boyfriend had seemed like her world. She didn't feel that now. Didn't a man as special as Giff deserve that kind of devotion, someone who would view him as her world?

You don't feel that because you've matured, *dummy.* Giff wanted a woman he could build a life with, not someone who mooned over him like an infatuated teenager.

"Never mind." Brooke scooted her chair back. "I'm not making any sense."

Kresley grinned. "If it makes you feel any better, I wasn't always coherent during my engagement, either. I swore I was going to lose my mind before the actual wedding arrived. Of course, I let Dane's mom and mine talk us into a huge circus of a wedding. You shouldn't have that problem."

"Definitely not," Brooke said, repressing a shudder at the idea of turning her ceremony into a spectacle. "Some people might find it weird that I write about all these gala weddings for a living and don't want one of my own, but my job's given me time to really think about it." People stressed over colors and fabrics and venues…which font to use on the invitations, for pity's sake!

But those were details. They weren't marriage. She felt as though 90 percent of her job was writing prologues instead of an actual story. People didn't seem to realize that the Big Day was nothing more than the once-upon-a-time part; they had years—decades—ahead of them to work toward their happily-ever-after.

Maybe she was cynical, but when she typed up stories of horse-drawn carriages and the release of white doves, she found herself wondering if the bride and groom weren't trying a bit too hard, if they weren't compensating, substituting storybook-style romance for deeper, truer love. She and Giff might not revel in the glitz, but they had a good partnership.

She smiled, her spirits lifted. "If I'm going to take off early to meet Giff this afternoon, I'd better get to work."

"Absolutely." Kresley made shooing motions toward the door. "Go earn your keep."

Brooke's day passed quickly; she typed up two engagement announcements, had a phone interview with a local woman starting her own greeting card line and drafted a story about a bride and groom who planned to work both of their very different heritages into the ceremony. Was it hubris that she thought it turned out to be a very touching article?

When the phone rang after lunch, she answered it with a smile, half-expecting Giff. They were supposed to look at three wedding venues today.

"This is Brooke Nichols." Soon to be Brooke Baker. She rolled the name around in her head, adjusting to the sound of it. Unfortunately her pleasant musing was cut short by a mother of the bridezilla who was calling to complain that her daughter's marriage to a young man from Conroe hadn't received more coverage.

And I thought the bride was shrill. Brooke held the phone a few inches away from her ear and kicked herself for not leaving ten minutes ago.

After she'd finally escaped the haranguing, Brooke had to call Giff and warn him that she'd be slightly late for their meeting at the country club.

He laughed. "Good. Makes me feel better. I'm about fifteen minutes behind myself. I got blindsided with a client crisis."

"Which you no doubt solved," she said loyally.

"Unfortunately, no. I'm going to drive down to Corpus Christi tonight so that I can meet with them first thing in the morning. But I should be back tomorrow in plenty of time for the concert."

The tickets had been an early birthday gift from Meg, and Brooke had been touched that, this year, Meg had bought her something absolutely perfect. Instead of, say, the leather halter top Meg had given her six years ago, then promptly asked to borrow.

Brooke loved music of all types. If she and Giff were having a larger wedding, she would have wanted a live band for the reception. Her favorite part of wedding reporting was probably the musical choices—whether there was a string quartet, organ player, recorded music or even bagpipes. The song chosen for the father-daughter dance. The song the bride walked down the aisle to— nothing wrong with the traditional Wedding March, she supposed, but a lot of women went with selections from Vivaldi or Handel. *Or Zeppelin.* In one of the weddings she'd written about last year, the bridal processional had been accompanied by "Stairway to Heaven."

She tried to imagine what she herself would use but drew a blank. Probably because she didn't yet have an aisle to walk down. After today, they should be closer to resolving that issue.

The country club's event coordinator, Gretchen, was a petite woman with such big hair that Brooke wondered how she got through the day without toppling over. Gretchen's cheerful reminder that the venue had a capacity of up to 450 wasn't exactly a selling point.

"What is she not understanding about an intimate ceremony?" Brooke whispered to Giff.

"My problem," he returned under his breath, "isn't that it's too big. It's too distracting. It overlooks the twelfth hole—half the male guests will be thinking it's a pretty day to hit the greens. And I don't really want golf carts zooming by the window while we exchange vows."

The next place, a community hall built nearly forty years ago and available for rental, didn't feel quite right, either. In addition to a giant Lone Star flag covering the top quarter of one wall, the decor included some hunting trophies with eyes that seemed to follow Brooke wherever she moved.

"It's quaint," Giff told the leasing agent. "I can absolutely see having a large birthday party here or a corporate barbecue, but it seems a bit rustic for the wedding." On the walk out to his Lexus, he added for Brooke's ears only, "I kept imagining you in a cowboy hat with a bridal veil attached."

"Which do exist," she confirmed. "But I hadn't planned on wearing one."

Their third option, a pretty bed-and-breakfast, was closest to what Brooke had imagined, but Giff seemed ambivalent when they promised the manager they'd get back to her.

"Are you sorry we can't use your church?" Brooke asked.

The Baker family had been longtime members of a Methodist church near Grace's house, but according to the church's wedding coordinator, they were booked through winter.

"Not really." He looked pensive as he opened the passenger door for her. Once he'd climbed in on his own side, he added, "The last major family event there was my dad's funeral. I hate that you never got a chance to meet him. He would have liked you."

"I'm sure I would have liked him, too." There was a sudden knot in Brooke's throat. Not for the first time since she'd started dating Giff, it occurred to her that, while her parents might not be perfect, they loved her and they were healthy. She was lucky to have them.

"I know it's been years since my dad died," Giff said, sounding abashed that it had an effect on him even now, "but…"

"He was your father. It's natural that you'd still miss him, especially on a day as important as your wedding."

Giff nodded. "When Mom got sick, I missed him more than ever. There were times I didn't know what to say to her, when I was sure he would have found a way to comfort her, and when I thought that I might lose them both…."

Reaching over, Brooke squeezed his hand. "She's doing great now. And you have me. You're not alone."

He flipped the key in the ignition, his voice becoming determinedly cheerful. "I can't tell you how excited Mom is about these wedding preparations. She was touched that you invited her to go dress shopping with you. She's been downright giddy, happier than I've seen her in a long time. In fact…"

"Yes?"

"Nothing. Just thinking out loud," he mumbled.

Brooke grinned at him. "'Out loud' is when you actually say the words."

"Well, I'd need to talk to Mom about it. And we'd need to sit down with a tentative guest list to see how small a group we're both really comfortable with. But… maybe we could be married at home. Her home, where I grew up."

"That sounds perfect." Brooke couldn't imagine what it would have been like to have a true home, being raised in one place.

She and her family had bounced across states, through jobs, school districts and less-than-successful business ventures. She'd lived in houses, apartments and extended-stay hotels. But that had been Brooke Nichols.

Brooke Baker was putting down roots.

Chapter Five

Jake answered his phone Friday morning to the worst Brando impression he'd ever heard: "'Some day...I will call upon you to do a service for me.'"

"Giff?" Jake put a hand over his ear to block out the background noise from the fire station.

"Sorry, I flipped on the hotel TV last night and stumbled across a *Godfather* marathon," Giff said by way of explanation. "I need a favor."

"Name it."

"You working tonight?"

"No, I'm coming off a twenty-four-hour shift." Some of the rookies complained about them, unable to get any worthwhile sleep in the downtime between calls, but in the military Jake had perfected his ability to get whatever shut-eye he could wherever he could. "I'm scheduled to leave in a few hours and come back tomorrow. What do you need?"

"A date. For Brooke."

The image of the brunette from the other night's dinner came swiftly to mind, and it was a picture of contradictions. She was a lush, vibrant-looking woman who didn't seem to fit her own skin. With her generous mouth and choice of bright yellow clothing, she seemed like someone who should laugh loudly and enjoy some boldly uninhibited hobby. Skinny-dipping, maybe. *Whoa.* Before his mind could go somewhere as inappropriate as Giff's fiancée, unclothed, Jake did a mental edit. Salsa-dancing. That was safe.

But from the vibes she'd put off Wednesday, she was too stiff to salsa. Her demeanor would have just as easily fit a too-skinny woman with a pinched expression and a smile that didn't reach her eyes. *Obviously Brooke isn't that bad. If she was, Giff wouldn't be with her.*

"You still there?" Giff asked.

"I'm here, but I'm confused. I'm pretty sure *you're* signed up to be Brooke's date for life. The best man gets called in when there are single, good-looking bridesmaids who need to be squired around."

"I'm stuck in Corpus on business, and I was supposed to go with Brooke to a concert tonight. Her sister got her tickets, and Brooke's really been looking forward to it."

"Maybe the sister can go?" Jake suggested. *Anyone but me.*

"Meg waitresses. No way she can get a Friday night off at the last minute. Look, you and I both know Brooke could probably come up with someone, but you owe me. For that debacle at Comida Buena."

Jake winced, recalling the look on Giff's face— made worse only by Brooke's appalled expression. "I never meant for her to hear that." He had to admit, though, she'd handled the situation with more grace than he would have predicted. In spite of her smile being strained for the rest of the evening, she'd taken the high road and largely forgiven him without actually making him apologize. Whether he owed Giff or not, it seemed that he owed Brooke Nichols.

"All right" he heard himself say. "I can escort her to this concert. Assuming she's in favor of it?" Frankly he couldn't imagine she was in a big hurry to see him again, but maybe she'd agreed to the conciliatory gesture as a favor to Giff, just as Jake had.

"About that," Giff hedged. "I wanted to check and make sure you were even free before I bothered her with the idea. Let's do this—if she's averse to going with you, I'll leave you a message. If you don't hear back from me, pick her up by seven. The show's in the city and begins at eight. And, Jake, I really want the two of you to get along. Give her a chance, get to know each other. Be charming, damn it."

"Charming?" That had never been a problem before, especially with an attractive female. While she wasn't his type, even he conceded that Brooke Nichols was beautiful. "Yeah, I can do that."

BROOKE HAD JUST FINISHED checking her reflection over her shoulder—just because you *could* zip up and wear a pair of snug jeans didn't always mean you *should*— when the doorbell rang. She felt the smile stretch across her face. Tickets in her purse, her wonderful fiancé at the door; not even eight o'clock, and it was already a great night. She swung the door open wide in welcome.

The smile froze on her face, feeling like some

frostbitten appendage that might snap in half at any second. "J-Jake?"

Jake McBride, in a dark blazer and matching slacks, stood on her front porch. His eyes narrowed. "He didn't tell you, did he?"

"Wh…?" The unintelligible syllable was all she could manage. It had been bad enough being ambushed with Jake "July" McBride the first time. *What is he doing here?* "I was expecting Gifford." She fell back on formality as her ingrained antidote to nerves.

"Yeah, I was reaching that conclusion. He called me earlier today and asked me to take you to the concert." With a sweeping glance from her red, gauzy, V-necked top to her black jeans, he added, "I may have gotten the wrong idea about what kind of concert."

Brooke barely heard him. She was too busy sucking in her breath and asking questions of an absent Giff. *Gifford, love of my life, man who's supposed to know me better than anyone, did you just purposely sic a surprise on me?* Even impetuous Meg had learned better than that. Maybe if she actually spoke to Giff, his actions would seem more reasonable.

It would probably be rude to leave his best friend waiting on her porch while she tried to reach him. "Come on in," she offered, sounding only slightly less enthusiastic than she'd been about having her wisdom teeth removed last year.

Within seconds, she had her cell phone out of her purse, and was listening to the ring of Giff's phone. And then his voice mail. Probably because he was busy holding a client's hand, she told herself. Not because he was avoiding her. Giff was far too gallant for that kind of behavior.

"No luck?" McBride asked from behind her. "I promise, I'm here at his request."

"But *why?*" She was still trying to wrap her mind around Giff sending his friend with no warning. Obviously her fiancé wanted his closest friend and bride-to-be to make nice. "Never mind. I get it."

Jake rocked back on his heels. "We don't have to go together. I can see you're not exactly...thrilled by the idea."

"Which is weird," she said, wide-eyed, "because normally I love spending time with people who think I'm a big mistake." Her response startled her. Having grown up with people who never censored themselves—and having witnessed the fallout that usually resulted—Brooke tended to guard her words more carefully and repress sarcastic tendencies.

"Ouch." Jake pressed a hand to his chest as if wounded, but he didn't seem angry. "I can see where I might have had that coming. I'm...sorry if I hurt your feelings the other day. It really wasn't about you, though. I have a long-standing history of trying to look out for Giff."

She nodded. "I've heard how the two of you met. And loyalty's an admirable trait. But it's not like he's a scrawny fourth-grader anymore."

"Yeah. He's a rich, successful man."

Her fingers tightened around her cell phone, which she admirably didn't throw at his head. "Are you implying that I'm some kind of gold digger?"

Instead of answering, he glanced around her sparsely furnished, low-budget apartment. It was all right—clean and conveniently situated to give her access in Houston without living there—but more suited to the two twentysomething girls downstairs who had retail jobs at the nearby Katy Mills Mall and took classes at University of Houston System's Cinco Ranch campus. This wasn't where a thirty-year-old settled with her husband and raised children.

"I'm not poor," she blurted.

His eyes warmed with amusement. "I didn't say you were."

"I know this place isn't fancy. I've been saving up." Not needing much space for just herself, she'd regarded this apartment as simply a way station. Even before she'd started seeing Giff, she'd had The Plan: Meet a great guy, eventually move into a house where they would make a real home together, build a family. Had she been more invested in that nebulous future than sprucing up her present?

"Very sensible of you," McBride said. "The apartment's...nice enough. Maybe a little bland. Not that I have room to talk. I haven't done anything with my house, either. It's a stereotype, but I thought women got into decorating more."

She planned to, eventually. Painting a nursery, wallpapering a kitchen where she'd prepare romantic anniversary dinners and before-school breakfasts. But she didn't know Jake well enough to explain how she'd been waiting her whole life for that dream home, the domestic nesting fantasies that had come to mean so much to her.

Instead of confiding her secrets, she shrugged. "Bland. I guess that's me."

His gaze locked with hers. "I wouldn't say that."

She swallowed, not sure what to say, not even sure whether he was paying her a compliment. Unfortunately the silence stretched too long. They looked at each other far too long. The moment became—*charged*—awkward.

He had truly amazing eyes.

"Brooke? What did you decide? You want to brush me off and go to your concert alone, or let me take you?"

It's for Giff, she reminded herself, the man who was helping make all her dreams come true and good-naturedly tolerated her family. Two weeks ago, Meg had decided to tail him around downtown in an effort to put to use what she was learning in her P.I. class; Giff had laughed about it rather than express concern that insanity ran in Brooke's DNA. The least she could do was show the same acceptance for the people in his life.

"Let's go," she said. "Who knows? It might even be fun."

His lips twitched at her undisguised doubt. "Your car or mine?"

As unsettled as she was feeling, it was probably wise to let him drive. No point in risking lives and making herself look stupid by running a stoplight or something. "Yours, if that's okay." She followed him down the stairs.

"Sure." He pointed beneath one of the parking lights. "I'm right there."

It was a small, fuel-efficient hybrid. Brooke blinked. "That's your car?"

"Yeah." He glanced back at her. "Why? What were you expecting?"

The man oozed testosterone. She hadn't really given his vehicle preference any thought, but if someone had asked her to hazard a guess, she probably would have said a sports car. Or a pickup truck.

McBride's smile was at her expense, but that made it no less enticing. "You want to sit up front with me, or are your preconceived notions riding shotgun?"

"You're one to talk," she said without heat, knowing he had a point. "Did you even wait until I walked into the restaurant Wednesday before you decided I was a money-grubbing mistake, or had you deduced that the second he told you he was engaged?"

"Touché." He stopped to open the door for her, reminding her oddly of Giff. So far, the two men seemed much more different than similar.

As soon as Jake slid into the driver's seat, he said, "I overreacted when Giff told me he'd proposed. It just seemed—to an outsider—like this was happening awfully fast. And it occurred to me that a woman infatuated with his wealth might be in position to take advantage of his vulnerability. It devastated him to think he might lose Grace."

"I know," she said softly, grudgingly touched by Jake's concern for his friend even if it had caused him to judge her harshly. She recalled Giff's words yesterday about how excited his mom was about the wedding plans and how relieved he was to see her so happy and energetic.

"I was rooming with him in college when he lost his dad. It…" Jake shook his head. "Like I said earlier, I think I'm just in the habit of trying to look out for him. Even when there's nothing I can actually do."

Feeling powerless was never easy for anyone, but she imagined that for a big, tough guy like Jake—a man whose profession actually sent him into burning buildings to save lives—the feeling of not being able to act was excruciating. Something inside her softened and she found that, contrary to her expectations, she might come to like this guy after all.

"Brooke?"

"Yeah?"

"You're going to have to direct me here. I don't have a clue where we're going."

"THANKS AGAIN FOR AGREEING to drive," Brooke said as they searched for parking. "The traffic and the freeways here make me crazy. I have to say, even though I know it makes sense to move in with Giff I'm not looking forward to driving this close to downtown."

"No problem." City-driving in Houston wasn't Jake's favorite pastime, either, but navigating all kinds of streets came with his job. "I'm just glad you knew how to get to this place. I've never heard of it."

Her smile was lopsided, almost self-deprecating. "It's a total hole-in-the-wall. You should have seen Giff's face the first time I dragged him here. But they get some great bands that aren't well-enough known to book bigger venues."

"Like the band we're hearing tonight?"

"Red Jump Funk. They're a little under the radar," she admitted. "They're fantastic, though."

"They sound like a mad-lib," he said as he parallel parked between a VW and a truck. "You know those stories where you fill in random verbs and adjectives? How did you even hear about these people?"

"It's a hobby," she said as she opened her car door. "My favorite part of living in Austin was the music."

He grinned, shrugging out of the blazer he'd realized was unnecessary. "Just from my few visits, I do have some fond memories of clubs on Sixth Street."

"I dated a guy who followed some great underground bands—people no one else had ever heard of. But he was more of a reverse snob than I turned out to be. In his opinion, anyone who had more than a hundred fans worldwide was a sellout. But I love music of all kinds. I saw lots of people perform live during my college years." Either Brooke was nervous about being out with him tonight, or she was truly passionate about the topic of music because as she made her way up the sidewalk, her words came faster, practically tripping over one another. "Ska bands, Robert Earl Keen Jr., Leonard Cohen, Crüxshadows. They're a dark-wave group I love."

Dark wave? Was that like Goth? Once you got past the pinched smiles and barren apartment, Brooke Nichols got a lot more interesting. He had a sudden discordant image of Brooke in heavy eyeliner and a surprisingly appealing black leather skirt. He was appalled to find that his gaze had slid downward to her denim-encased hips. In her eagerness to get to tonight's show, she was walking with a noticeable bounce in her step.

"So how long did you date the reverse snob?" he asked, jerking his head up. "Was it serious?"

She was silent for a minute, and he wondered if she'd even heard the question. Or might at least be pretending not to have heard.

Then she admitted over her shoulder, "Next to Giff, the most serious relationship I've ever had. And one of the worst mistakes I've ever made in my life."

He was intrigued, but figured he'd already pried enough. Her past affairs were really none of his business. Besides, they were coming up on a group of people that he realized actually represented a disorganized line on the sidewalk. Clusters of three and four people stood talking and laughing in the mottled illumination of streetlights and neon signs.

"I take it we're here?" he asked her.

She turned and nodded, looking so happy that Jake felt bad for his buddy. Giff was missing out. From the flush in her cheeks and sparkle in her blue eyes to the hint of cleavage revealed by her red shirt, Brooke was undeniably sexy tonight. Which was completely wasted on him.

"Thanks for being such a good sport," he told her. "About having to come with me. I know plenty of women who would be ticked if their boyfriends stood them up because of work."

Brooke looked genuinely shocked. "I have nothing but respect for how hard Giff works. I know he inherited money from his dad. Some people would have used that as an excuse to be lazy, but Giff would never do that. He's the kind of man who will always provide for his family."

While Jake could admit he'd jumped to conclusions about Brooke possibly being social-climbing opportunist infatuated with Giff's bank account, he couldn't help noticing how fervent she sounded when she talked about Giff supporting a family. He supposed it was normal for a potential mother to want her future children to be well taken care of, but her tone seemed bizarrely intent. How much insecurity had she experienced during her own childhood?

They blended into the free-form line, awaiting their turn to show ID and give their tickets to the broad-shouldered men at the door. His first glance at the interior bore out her earlier description that it was a hole-in-the-wall. The club—and he used the term generously—might only be a few miles away from the more popular bars over on Westheimer, like the Bull & Bear, Catbirds or Privé, but it was worlds removed from them in terms of atmosphere and polish.

This place was characterized by dim lighting, a concrete floor and extremely limited seating. There were some stools at the bar and a few tall tables scattered throughout. Since a lot of people were crowded onto the dance floor or in line for a drink, he and Brooke were able to snag a two-person table to the left of the stage. An opening act was already playing. The music wasn't remarkable, but the drums provided a strong rhythm for those dancing.

Jake spoke loudly over the beat. "Can I get you something to drink?"

"Whatever light beer they've got on draft is fine." She gave him a wide smile, surprising him with a previously hidden dimple. "I tried a glass of wine here once and won't be making that mistake again. I wouldn't *cook* with that stuff."

By the time he'd returned with their beers, the opening band had finished its set and people in the crowd were beginning to chant for the headliners. The room was dark for a second, then a lone spotlight came up on a tall woman—her height boosted by the wickedly heeled boots she wore—with waist-length red hair. He wondered if she was the Red in the group's name. She filled the club with the sound of an electronic violin and was joined by a guitarist, keyboardist and lead singer. Their lyrics were strangely melancholy, considering the funky toe-tapping quality of the music.

Brooke, clearly familiar with the band's work, was singing along, wriggling and swaying in her chair.

He leaned close to make himself heard, wondering if it would be inappropriate to tell her she smelled really good. "I guess if Giff were here, the two of you would be dancing?"

Angling her head, she looked at him, her blue eyes unreadable. Then she laughed. "Not likely. Giff doesn't dance."

Jake had a memory of Giff's high school girlfriend trying to cajole him out onto the floor at their senior prom. "What about you, Brooke? You dance?"

The answer was obviously yes. Even seated, she was all but shimmying to the music.

"I…used to. But not in years," she added, sounding nervous. "I'm way out of practice."

"Well, what are we waiting for?" He held out a hand. "No time like the present, right?"

Chapter Six

This is bad. Dancing with her fiancé's best friend shouldn't feel so good, Brooke admonished herself. But maybe it had nothing to do with the guy in front of her; maybe it was just the uninhibited thrill of dancing again. Her old boyfriend Sean had told her once that he'd known they'd be incredible together in bed after seeing her on a dance floor. *The way you moved,* he'd said. No one had ever said anything so erotic to her.

She frowned, dismissing the memory. No amount of "incredible" had made that relationship worth saving. He'd been erratic and moody, as undependable in the long run as she'd found him sexy in the short term.

The opportunity to cut loose on a dance floor tonight, combined with her enjoyment of the band really did make this the best present Meg had ever given her. *I have to remember to call and thank her.* Or not. Brooke could just imagine trying to explain to her sister—who found a way to make even the most innocent situations sound suggestive—that she'd spent her Friday night dancing with Giff's hunky friend.

It wasn't as if this kind of music lent itself to ballroom

dancing; Jake didn't have an arm around her waist and shoulder. They were only dancing "together" in a loose interpretation of the word. Then again, given the limited space in the club and the active enthusiasm of the crowd around her, she'd found herself jostled against him more than enough times to appreciate his fireman's muscles beneath the button-down shirt he wore.

After half an hour, she realized she was getting too breathless to sing along and that her calves and thighs were getting the slightest bit sore. *Not twenty anymore.*

"I think I need to sit for a minute," she admitted.

"Want anything else to drink?"

She nodded vehemently. "Bottle of water. Please."

No sooner had she returned to their table than the band slowed down for one of the few ballads in their repertoire. Brooke felt a wave of relief that she and Jake hadn't still been on the dance floor when the first notes of the love song had played. That would have been awkward.

Although, come to think of it, despite their rocky start to the evening, tonight had been far less awkward than she'd anticipated. He had a good sense of humor, seemed to be enjoying himself and was inarguably easy on the eyes—all in all, a fun companion. Her earlier irritation with Giff had long since faded, although it still puzzled her that someone who knew her so well would spring a surprise on her.

"Your water, ma'am." Jake handed over the cold bottle with a flourish.

"You are officially my hero," she said, twisting off

the cap. "I'll be petitioning the city to put up a statue in your honor."

"It wouldn't be the first," he drawled.

She laughed but realized that he probably *had* performed more than his fair share of heroics. "So, you're a fireman." A noble job, but she couldn't imagine how scary it could be—both for the person doing it and their loved ones.

"And a paramedic. More and more first responders—the full-time guys called to emergencies, rather than part-time backups or community volunteers—function in dual roles these days."

"You've probably saved lives." It made the trivial aspects of her job—like reporting on the color of flowers in a bouquet—seem silly.

He fidgeted, looking more uncomfortable than she'd ever seen him. Even more so than he'd been Wednesday when he realized she'd overheard his less than flattering opinion of her engagement. "Yeah, well, all part of the job. I'm not— I've seen guys risk their lives for other people lots of times, make sacrifices that I…"

Was he talking about his time in the military?

"I can't quite envision you in the army," she said. Being a soldier was the epitome of structure. "Isn't that an odd fit for someone who prefers the freedom to go wherever the spirit moves him?"

He rolled his bottled soft drink between his palms, not meeting her eyes. "Joining the service provided me with a lot. Financial help with college, but also less tangible benefits."

"Such as?" she prompted.

"My childhood was turbulent. In contrast, there were some aspects of rigid military structure that appealed to me."

Brooke blinked. She hadn't been expecting to find much common ground with Jake McBride, but it sounded as if they'd both had unpredictable upbringings. "We used to move around a lot. My parents changed jobs constantly. Well, Dad, anyway. Mom had a few temp positions and some failed creative endeavors. Nothing you could call steady." Steadiness had never been a priority in the Nichols household.

"My mother worked two jobs," Jake said. "Partly because we needed the money, but partly, I think, because it got her out of the house and away from my father. He was a cop once, a long time ago, and I remember wanting to be just like him. Then he got injured on the job—shot—and wound up drinking through most of his disability pay."

"That must have been hard on all of you."

"I survived," Jake said, but his grim tone made it clear he hadn't survived unscathed.

As she finished her water, Brooke studied him discreetly. It didn't look as if he wanted to go into more detail about his past, but she found herself so curious about him. How had he moved from wanting the discipline of the army to becoming the man Giff described as Mr. Spontaneity? Had it been difficult, befriending the wealthy Giff, with his doting parents, when Jake himself came from a family that was struggling to make ends meet while coping with a bitter ex-cop's drinking problem?

She settled on a neutral question. "Do your mother and father still live in the area?"

"Yeah." He crumpled his empty plastic bottle. "I'm done with my drink, if you want to dance some more."

"Sure, okay." She followed him out to the throng of people, trying to pick up the gyrating pulse of the music. At first she had trouble recapturing the fluid grace she'd felt earlier. Mostly she moved her torso in a slightly off-tempo sway and mumbled an apology whenever she bumped someone.

Eventually, however, her panacea kicked in—music had always worked as a temporary cure for what ailed her, including sudden clumsiness with a man who'd revealed more about himself than he'd intended. By the time the Funk took the stage for their encore, she was caught back up in the song, momentarily forgetting everything else around her.

When the band bid the audience a final goodbye, she turned to Jake with a smile. "Thanks for bringing me. I needed this tonight."

"My pleasure," he said. "I enjoyed myself."

Even though the May temperature was warm, the night air was refreshing after the sweaty confines of the club. Brooke closed her eyes and inhaled deeply. She realized that Jake was humming one of the band's songs under his breath.

"So you really liked the music?" she asked.

"Absolutely. And I appreciate your not laughing at me on the dance floor."

Laugh? She'd been awed that a man with his muscular

build moved with such silky grace. Rather than admit that, she said, "It's been a long time since I went dancing. You forget that it's real exercise. I worked up an appetite."

"I could go for a bite to eat," he agreed. "You know of any places around here?"

"There's a little Italian diner that stays open late on the weekends. It's too far to walk, but it's on our way to the freeway."

During the ride, they discussed music he liked, including a couple of Danish bands some of his well-traveled army buddies had played for him. The short drive passed quickly, and Brooke was so engrossed in their conversation that she almost forgot to watch for their turn. As they entered the restaurant, Brooke thought about all of the wedding dresses she would be trying on tomorrow. She should probably get a Greek salad with grilled chicken and light dressing. But as soon as the smell of pepperoni and melted cheese wafted over her, she knew she was a goner.

Succumbing to temptation, she asked for a calzone. Jake ordered a bowl of tortellini after she'd assured him everything here was great.

"I'm going to regret this," she said after their waiter walked away. "A calzone is not exactly health food."

"Live a little," Jake chided.

"Easy for you to say. You won't be spending tomorrow trying to zip yourself into white satin and taffeta. Grace and I are going wedding dress shopping," she clarified. Her mouth quirked in teasing smile. "At least,

I assume my date with Grace still stands and that I won't open my door to find you again?"

"No, I'll be sleeping in, then reporting back to the station. A shame really, because there are worse ways to spend a day than telling a beautiful woman what makes her look good." As if realizing how flirtatious that had sounded, he straightened abruptly. "So…shopping with Grace? Not your own mom?"

"Tomorrow is just the initial search. When I have it narrowed down to a few specific options, I'll bring along my mom and sister." Was there a diplomatic way to admit that she tolerated them best in small doses? "And it gives me a chance to bond with my future mother-in-law."

"Grace is a wonderful woman. She was a second mother to me," he said fondly. "I hated being so far away when she was sick."

"Is that why you decided to leave the Army?" Brooke asked. "To be closer to loved ones?"

"My term was up. I was ready to come home. Besides… You know how I said that I was initially drawn to the disciplined lifestyle?"

She nodded in complete understanding. Routine was soothing. There was a lot to be said for waking up in the morning and knowing what the day ahead held in store.

"I grew up a lot during my time in the service. I realized that order can be a crutch. Don't get me wrong—in the military there's a reason for such structure. It's the same for firefighters. Following procedure saves lives. I get that, and adhere to it at work. But in the everyday, trying to pretend that life follows a safe, predefined pattern is just denial, if not outright cowardice."

"Cowardice?" The burgeoning warmth she'd been feeling at finding common ground cooled abruptly. "You make it sound like a weakness to want an orderly life, but the truth is, that takes effort and planning. Lazy people who can't be bothered to think ahead or stick to a plan try to gloss over their own character flaws by making themselves seem carefree!"

"Looks like I hit a nerve," he observed cautiously.

Her cheeks heated. "I…I wasn't trying to call you lazy. I grew up in a very 'spontaneous' household."

"You?"

"I was the token which-of-these-things-is-not-like-the-others," she mumbled.

"Ah."

"It's not like I'm insane. I don't have my DVDs alphabetized or my socks inventoried or anything."

"That thought never crossed my mind," he assured her with a grin.

Maybe it was better if she shut up and just ate. Except that the waiter hadn't brought their plates out yet. Given this example of her scintillating conversation with the opposite sex, it was amazing she'd ever got a guy like Giff to ask her out on a date, much less propose. Except it wasn't like this with Giff. She didn't stumble over her words or find herself bizarrely defensive. He was as comfortable as a favorite bathrobe, a perfect fit.

As if she'd mentally conjured their food through sheer desperation, the waiter appeared.

"Wow," Jake said when he got his first look at the calzone. "That's... Wow."

"You're the one who told me to live a little!" She could always work this off. If she hired a personal trainer and replaced her full-time job with forty-plus hours a week in the gym.

"Yeah, but that's before I saw the thing. It's big enough to have its own gravitational pull. It's a *planet*."

She mock-glared at him. "It is not."

"Close enough." He snapped his fingers. "It's like Pluto. You know how it was a planet back when we were in school but got demoted? What is it now? The planet formerly known as Pluto."

She stifled a giggle, not wanting to sound like a teenage girl. "I am officially ignoring you so I can eat."

He dug into his own not-insubstantial bowl of tortellini, and she managed to finish three quarters of the calzone. When the waiter handed Jake the check, she shook her head.

"You should let me pay," she insisted. "You bought drinks at the club. At least let's go halves?"

"Nah, you can pick it up next time," he told her.

Next time? The thought caused a flutter of apprehension. Despite having had more fun tonight than she could have anticipated, she wasn't planning to make a habit of alone time with Jake McBride. It would be too... It just wasn't a prudent idea.

"Maybe we could double-date sometime," she suggested. "Me and Giff, you and..."

"I'm not seeing anyone right now."

"Not for a lack of female admirers, I'm sure."

Certainly *she* would never consider a relationship with someone like Jake, with his frequent footloose jaunts and a career that involved leaping into dangerous situations. He was the Anti-Giff! But plenty of women would look past that, might even find it sexy.

When he raised a brow at her, she rolled her eyes. "Oh, come on. You own a mirror, don't you?"

He laughed. "Thanks. I think."

"So there's really no one you're interested in?" She told herself she was just exhibiting friendly curiosity. This was what Giff had wanted, right? For her to get to know Jake better? But she couldn't deny that she wanted Jake to have a girlfriend. It would make things more... symmetrical if he were attached.

You could always introduce him to Meg. She'd eat him up with a spoon. But no sooner had the thought occurred to her than her stomach clenched and she rejected the idea. Meg and Jake would practically be in-laws after the wedding, and when they broke up—which they would since Meg's relationships never lasted—it might make holidays and family gatherings awkward.

"I have a really erratic schedule at the station," he said. "I work multiple twenty-four-hour shifts in a row, plus swap shifts with other guys who have kids with baseball games and that sort of thing. Not all girlfriends want to put up with that. And I'm out of town a lot, so I haven't really been going out of my way to meet someone in my spare time."

"Giff mentioned your traveling." It was one of the reasons she'd never met Jake before this week. "Where do you go?"

"Anywhere. Everywhere. One of the things I discovered about myself in the army was that I love seeing new places. New places that aren't in the Middle East," he clarified as they rose to leave. "I went to Abbeville, Louisiana, for the cooking of a five-thousand-egg omelet."

Five *thousand* eggs? The mind boggled.

"I've gambled aboard Mississippi riverboat casinos, been climbing and rappelling in Denver. My latest trip was to New Mexico. I have some vacation time saved up for this summer and want to get to Hawaii. And in the fall, I'd like to take a quick trip up to New England. Even if it's only for a day, I want to see the leaves."

"Not much autumn color in Houston, is there?" she commiserated.

"I also like meeting new people," he said, holding open the restaurant door for her. "And I don't know that many women who can knowledgeably discuss Scandinavian rock bands *and* eat calzones bigger than their heads. You're full of surprises, Brooke."

"That's ironic," she said with a rueful smile over her shoulder. "Because I'm not a big fan of surprises."

"That's okay." He winked at her. "I like them enough for both of us."

Chapter Seven

Brooke had just stepped out of the shower Saturday morning when she heard her phone ring. "Hello?"

"Did you get my message last night?" Giff asked, his tone sheepish.

"I did." When Jake had dropped her off after their late dinner, she'd found a lengthy apology on her answering machine. Giff had admitted that it had been calculated on his part, waiting until late in the day to ask her to go with Jake because he was afraid that if she had more notice, she might demur and invite someone like Kresley instead. But then he'd been swept up into meetings and hadn't realized until later that night that he'd never given her a heads-up.

"So, did the two of you end up going to the concert together?"

"Yeah. And, I admit, we had fun." She started to say that his friend was a heck of a dancer, but second-guessed herself at the last instant.

Giff sighed, clearly relieved. "Does that mean you'll forgive me my isolated, never-to-be-repeated Machiavellian moment? I'm on the way back to Houston now and fully prepared to grovel in person."

She laughed. "No groveling necessary. How about you just promise not to ambush me again?"

"Absolutely. I wouldn't normally have done that, you know. I just— He's a good guy. I wanted to give you a chance to see that side of him."

"Well, mission accomplished. Now, if you'll excuse me, I have thirty minutes to get presentable for your mom. Which is going to be a stretch since I'm currently dripping wet and wearing a towel."

"All right, I'll see you tomorrow."

Brooke was looking forward to supper at Grace's, which she predicted would be blissfully normal, entirely unlike the evening Giff had first met her parents a month ago. The Nichols had invited Meg and her then-boyfriend over for dinner and once Didi realized that her other daughter was also seeing someone, she'd insisted Brooke and Giff join them. Everett had tried to impress everyone with an experimental dish, but let his perfectionist temperament get in the way—declaring the meal too flawed to serve. So they'd had to wait an additional forty minutes for pizza to be delivered, during which time Meg's boyfriend had insisted on performing for them. He'd juggled several of Didi's household knick-knacks, inadvertently breaking a trophy she'd prized from a long-ago dance competition. To be fair to the juggler, he'd had three drinks on an empty stomach while waiting for the promised food. Probably he was better at his job when sober.

I should have proposed to Giff myself after that night,

Brooke thought as she stepped out of her apartment and locked the front door. Anyone who'd been as patiently amused and good-natured about his three hours with the Nichols family was a keeper. But then, that was Giff. Mr. Supportive. She was secure in the knowledge that whatever decisions she made, Giff would back them. The closest they'd ever come to a disagreement was his siccing Jake on her without warning, but even that had turned out well.

En route to her appointment at the first bridal boutique, Brooke slipped in the earpiece for her phone and dialed Kresley's number to give her an update.

"I may have spoken too soon about Giff's friend."

"The one who's the devil?"

"Exactly." Brooke flipped on her blinker and slid into the next lane. "I spent last night with him and—"

"What?"

"You know how Giff and I were going to the Red Jump Funk concert? He got tied up in Corpus and sent Jake in his stead. It was his guerrilla attempt to make us buddies."

"Sounds like it worked to some degree."

"Yeah. When he's not accusing me of marrying Giff for his money, Jake is fun to be around. And there's a lot more to him than I first realized." She thought about what it must have been like to grow up with an alcoholic father and the kinds of things Jake might have seen in his time overseas. Yet he was still quick with a teasing smile and quips that made her laugh.

"I have to say, this restores my faith in Giff," Kresley

said. "A great guy like him? It didn't make sense that his best friend would be a jerk."

After promising to e-mail snapshots of today's best dresses from her cell phone, Brooke disconnected, but her friend's words stuck with her.

Jake had definitely shown his gentlemanly side last night, but she still found aspects of his friendship with Giff puzzling. The business consultant who would be lost without his BlackBerry and the guy who was always disappearing on spontaneous road trips and declared structure cowardly? Maybe it was the "bromance" version of opposites attracting, people complementing each other's strengths and weaknesses.

Of course, when it came to dating, opposites didn't always attract. She and Giff were cut from the same cloth, but that just made it easier to lay the foundation for their marriage, knowing they wanted the same things out of life and wouldn't be working toward conflicting goals. Brooke had once been dazzled by someone utterly unlike her, but had learned from that youthful folly.

Sustaining relationships was difficult enough—why set yourself up for failure by falling for someone who had a fundamentally different outlook on life?

"WE MAY HAVE FOUND A WINNER." Grace beamed into the mirror, her eyes meeting Brooke's in their reflection. "You look stunning, dear."

"It's the dress," Brooke said. "This would make anyone look fabulous."

Grace laughed. "Untrue. Not everyone could pull off

that strapless look. But never mind about my opinion. What do *you* think of it?"

It seemed perfect, neither too fussy nor too blah. The strapless white dress had some subtle pleating at the bodice that added a touch of elegance without being busy; the gown flowed into an A-line skirt that was full without being puffy. Brooke had tried on—and quickly ruled out—two dresses this morning that made her feel like Little Bo Peep at a debutante ball. But understated beading trailed down the front of this dress, toward the scalloped floor-length hem, catching the light.

"Would you mind taking a picture for me?" Brooke asked absently, still studying the dress.

"Oh, my." The saleswoman, who'd disappeared up front to discuss flower girl dresses with another customer, had just returned. She smiled approvingly at the picture Brooke made atop the raised dais. "It looks tailor-made for you. Which is lucky since we don't have many size options. That dress has been discontinued, so I can give it to you for 40 percent off."

"Forty percent?" Brooke raised her eyebrows. She'd be a fool not to take it. She'd already thought it was reasonably priced, comparatively speaking.

"Talk about luck!" Grace said delightedly.

"Yeah. I was expecting this to take longer." Granted, they'd been at it all day and her feet were getting sore, but it did seem as though she'd stumbled into just the right dress pretty easily. Given the way all the details were falling into place with her and Giff's engagement, it was obviously meant to be.

Grace laughed. "It's a good thing it *didn't* take longer.

Now that you and Giff have set the date for mid-July, you don't have much time."

"July?" the sales lady echoed. "Not a second to lose, then!"

Still… "If I want to take a couple of days to think about it, maybe bring back my mom and sister for their input, can you put this on hold?" Brooke asked.

"We'll hold it for forty-eight hours, with a twenty-five dollar deposit."

The bell over the door rang, and the woman excused herself again. Grace snapped a couple of shots from different angles on Brooke's cell phone, so that she could send the images to Kresley. Afterward, Brooke meant to go put on her own clothes but instead found herself simply staring into the mirror.

"Brooke? Is everything all right, dear?"

"Yeah, I…" She trailed off because what she was thinking made no sense. If she said it aloud, Grace would need an explanation Brooke didn't think she could articulate. *I cannot picture myself in this dress.* Which, considering she was staring at that exact reflection, made her a candidate for the loony bin.

Well, the Nichols genes were bound to kick in sooner or later.

The dress was undoubtedly lovely. It was elegant enough for a bride marrying into the Baker family, casual enough for a small wedding and better suited to the summer heat than gowns with heavier beading or sleeves. But when she tried to envision it—her on her wedding day, wearing this, walking toward Giff and her future… Her mind remained frustratingly blank.

"Thanks for taking the pictures," Brooke finally said, "I should go get changed."

Taking a closer look at herself in the dressing room mirror, Brooke couldn't help but notice the circles under her eyes. Maybe that's why her thoughts weren't making much sense today—she'd been restless last night, tossing and turning, with songs from the concert stuck in her head. And Jake McBride in her thoughts.

Guilt immediately slammed into her conscience with the same tingling pain of an elbow against a wall. She tried to shake off the sensation. It wasn't that her thoughts had been disloyal to Giff; she hadn't been fantasizing about what it would be like to be with a man like Jake. She'd simply found herself recounting parts of their conversation and wondering about other aspects of his life. Taking an interest in a new acquaintance was not disloyal.

So why did she find it difficult to meet Grace's eyes when she stepped out of the fitting room?

"I don't know about you," Grace said, "but I could use a pick-me-up. I noticed a bakery on the corner when we came in. Want to go for a brownie or some cookies?"

"I'm not hungry, but I could use a hit of caffeine."

Inside, the little bakery was crowded to capacity. Grace and Brooke found seats out on the patio, beneath the shade of an oversize umbrella.

"You're sure you don't want half?" Grace asked, gesturing to her cheesecake brownie.

"Can't. I'm doing penance for a two-ton calzone from last night. But I promise to arrive for supper tomorrow ready to eat," Brooke said with a smile. "Giff tells me you're quite a cook."

Grace's already pleasant expression warmed even further at the mention of her only child. "He's such a good boy. A good man now. I'm ridiculously proud of him, you know."

"You have every right to be."

"And I'll be equally proud to call you my daughter-in-law. Brooke, there's something I want to do for you and Giff. Let me throw you an engagement party!"

"That's so generous. You're already letting us use the house for the wedding!" Brooke knew that Giff had approached his mom with the idea before heading to Corpus, wanting to give her a couple of days to think it over before she saw them tomorrow. But she'd agreed instantly, seeming overjoyed by the idea.

"I was touched when Giff said he wanted to be married there." Grace's blue eyes watered. "Some of my friends suggested that I sell the house when Giff's father died. With Giff already in college, it was more room than I really needed, but I just couldn't bring myself to do it. And now, he'll have his wedding there! And maybe, not too many years from now, there will be grandkids running around the yard and helping me bake Christmas cookies."

Brooke's own eyes turned misty. The vision Grace's words painted was exactly what Brooke herself had always wanted.

Grace sniffed. "Look at me! I swear, I never used to cry. And now I've turned into one of those women who can't get through a two-minute movie trailer without tearing up. No more maudlin talk! Back to the party—I know the two of you want an intimate wedding ceremony, but a big congratulatory bash would give other people a chance to offer their happy wishes as well."

Just how big was Grace thinking? "I don't want to put you to a lot of trouble," Brooke said slowly.

The older woman waved a hand. "I haven't had enough fun in the past two years, and I'm determined to make up for it. A joyous shindig is exactly what I need. And it's an opportunity to finally meet your family, in a fun setting."

There was something to be said for easing Grace slowly into a relationship with the Nichols, amid the buffer of other partygoers.

Brooke smiled gamely. "You've talked me into it."

Chapter Eight

Leaning back in her office chair, Brooke glared at the phone that had just started ringing. Again.

Between details she'd been writing up for other people's weddings, calls she'd been making about her *own* wedding and talking to Grace about this Friday's party, Brooke felt as if she hadn't been off the phone for more than five minutes in the past two and a half weeks. Some days she spent more time talking to Grace than Giff, although that didn't really bother her. After all, he was working harder than ever now to take a couple of weeks off after the wedding. *We have the next sixty or so years to talk—might as well pace ourselves.*

With a resigned sigh, she reached for the receiver. "The *Katy Chronicle*, Brooke Nichols speaking."

"Hey, sis. Is this a bad time?"

Depends, Brooke thought wearily, wondering if there was some new drama going on in Meg's life. Everything had seemed copacetic when they'd met to pick up Brooke's wedding dress, but that had been over a week ago and it didn't take Meg long to make drastic life changes. "I have a few minutes."

"I thought about not calling because you know how they are—it will probably blow over in the next forty-eight hours—but just in case, I decided it was only fair to warn you. I mean, this weekend is your engagement party, and I know you hate being caught off guard."

Brooke's stomach sank. "I'm going out on a limb here. Does your call have something to do with Mom and Dad?"

"She phoned me twenty minutes ago to ask if she can stay with me for a few nights. I told her sure, I mean what do I care, I work most nights anyway, but—"

"Megan." Brooke let just enough impatience seep into her voice to get her sister's attention.

"Right. Apparently they had a fight over an impulse buy."

Brooke groaned. Her mother, who had grown up in a household of seven children, had regaled them with stories of deprivation and complaints about how she'd always had to make do with hand-me-downs. Brooke had barely met her aunts and uncles, as Didi wasn't one for keeping in touch. Didi had taken off for Vegas as soon as she was legally old enough, hoping to follow her exotic dream of becoming a showgirl— She'd been told that she possessed raw talent as a dancer but was far too short. Though she'd been forced to abandon that aspiration, she'd doggedly clung to her resolve never to deny herself as an adult the way she'd been "deprived" as a child. Unfortunately her compulsive shopping issues did not mesh well with her husband's tendency to be between jobs.

This is all I need. Brooke tried to avoid making

situations all about her—that trait frequently got Didi and Meg into trouble—but the day after tomorrow, her parents were due to meet Grace for the first time. Brooke would prefer that the Nichols be on their best behavior. Luckily Meg had been able to get the night off for the party, so maybe she could help run interference—assuming she didn't get distracted by handsome partygoers.

"So Mom's coming to stay with you tonight?" Brooke clarified.

"Yeah, but like I said, I'll be at work."

"Do you mind if I stop by and talk with her?" Was there a diplomatic way to ask Didi to quit being a diva and avoid screwing up her youngest child's engagement party? *Probably not.*

"Be my guest." Meg's tone was tinged with apology. "I'd do it myself if I thought I could make her see reason, but that's always been more your specialty than mine. I'm sorry, Brooke. Just because you couldn't pay *me* to marry a businessman like Giff—no offense—doesn't mean I would try to sabotage any of this for you. I want your party and your wedding to be perfect."

Brooke was genuinely touched. "Thanks, sis. I'm sure that between the two of us we can get our parents to behave. And like you said, half of their fights blow over as quickly as they start." Which didn't stop Brooke from writing her parents' names on the notepad she kept handy for phone interviews, followed by a large *argh!* in Sharpie marker underneath.

No sooner had she hung up the phone than Kresley stuck her head through the doorway of the office.

"Hey." Brooke smiled. "Is there any chance your parents would want to adopt another adult daughter? They've always seemed like such lovely, well-adjusted people." *At least my future mother-in-law is organized and emotionally stable.*

Kresley, her expression concerned, didn't bother to address the facetious question. "Isn't Jake McBride the name of Giff's friend, the one you've been telling me about?"

"Yeah. Why?" Brooke studied her friend's troubled gaze and thought about the 911 scanner they kept in the newsroom. "Oh, God, was he in some kind of accident? Did—"

"No, he came across an accident this afternoon and jumped in to help. A little girl walking home from school had just been hit by an SUV." Kresley stopped, taking a shuddery breath. "Sorry. Any time a child is hurt is horrible, of course, but ever since I got pregnant, these things..."

"Is the girl okay?" Brooke asked hesitantly.

"She's in critical condition, but they credit Jake with keeping her alive until the ambulance arrived. We're running a story tomorrow, and I hope to God we have good news to report on her recovery. Apparently he was doing some kind of career day visit or something at the school and was coming from that direction, just like she was. She was unconscious and not breathing when he happened on the scene. He inserted an artificial airway, then helped the EMS team stabilize her on a spinal board."

Brooke's heart squeezed. Suddenly her ongoing

difficulty with mercurial parents seemed like the most trivial problem in the world. She couldn't imagine what that poor girl's family was going through.

"Anyway." Kresley leaned against the doorjamb, trying to steady herself with another deep breath. "I thought I recognized Jake's name. From what the ambulance driver said, Jake was the hero of the day."

"Then it's a blessing he was in the area." What kind of resilience did it take to weather a job where witnessing other people's trauma was the norm? Brooke suspected that the lives one was able to save made it worth it, but still...

As she started her short drive home, passing one of Katy's multiple parks where softball teams were practicing despite the heat, she found herself thinking about the emotional toll a job like Jake's could take on a person. Especially a person who seemed, in many ways, to be a loner. Whom did Jake confide in about difficult days and near misses? He'd said that he wasn't close to his family and didn't have a girlfriend.

On impulse, she dialed Giff's office, prepared to suggest he give Jake a call in case the other man needed a friendly ear. But about the time Brooke reached his voice mail, she remembered that he had dinner with a client tonight. He'd originally asked her if she would go with him, but when the client's wife was unable to make it, Giff had absolved Brooke of the obligation, admitting that conversation was bound to be pretty dry.

She'd passed by the fire station before and, relying on memory, found her way there with just two wrong turns. Would Jake even be there? *Only one way to find out.* She parked in a spot marked for guests and hurried out of her car before she changed her mind.

Would he think she was being intrusive or overre-acting? After all, this *was* his job. It was probable that he'd seen tragedies in the military, too. But then Brooke had a horrible vision of what it must have been like to see a child… Her mind skittered away from the image immediately, and she squared her shoulders. Whatever he thought, she knew she was right to be here. *He's a friend.* Or at the very least, a friend-in-law.

She walked inside a cramped front office where an auburn-haired woman in uniform was talking into a headset. The redhead smiled in Brooke's direction and held up her index finger.

A moment later, the woman hit a button on the tele-phone system in front of her and gave Brooke her full attention. "What can I do for you today?"

"I was looking for Jake McBride. I'm a friend." She held up her left hand so that her engagement ring was visible. "Giff Baker's fiancée."

The woman brightened at the mention of Giff's name. "That sweetheart wrote us a huge check when we were raising money for the children's burn unit last month. You tell him how much we all appreciate it. I think Jake's in the common room with some of the other guys. Just follow the blue-carpeted hallway to the first room on your left."

"Thanks." As she walked down the hall, Brooke heard male voices and tried to identify one of them as Jake's. None of them sounded familiar, though.

"Hello?" She peered into what looked like a living

room decorated in Early American Frat Boy. The couch was lumpy and faded to a dingy, indistinct color. There were two mismatched chairs and a coffee table with noticeable scuffs and water ring stains on its wooden surface. She suspected the entire furniture budget had gone toward the big-screen TV three men were watching.

At the sound of her voice, they all swiveled in her direction. The youngest man, with eyes nearly as dark a blue as his uniform, rose from his chair with a rakish grin. "Please make my day and tell me you're here to learn CPR."

"Hoskins, you dumbass, that's no way to talk to a lady." A fit-looking bald man threw an orange pillow at Hoskins, then glanced at Brooke sheepishly. "Sorry about the *dumbass,* ma'am."

She chuckled. "It's all right. But maybe one of you can help me? I was looking for Jake McBride."

All three men sobered. Hoskins grin faded, and he sounded far older when he answered, "He's in the back, ma'am, but he may not be up for visitors. I can check for you."

"I'd appreciate that. Can you let him know Brooke is here? Brooke Nichols."

"Will do."

The other two men exchanged a look. She couldn't tell exactly what they were thinking, but if she had to guess, she'd say they were worried about Jake. She'd overlooked these men earlier, she realized. She'd been concerned about Jake being a loner, but she hadn't taken into account that his fellow emergency workers had his back, probably a similar dynamic to what he'd experienced in the military. Had that also been part of the draw, an instant and loyal family of sorts for a boy who'd grown up with a rough home life?

"Brooke?"

She turned and nearly smacked into Jake, who was behind her. With Hoskins at his side, it was becoming very crowded in the small corridor. Jake wore the same dark uniform pants as the other men, but with only a white T-shirt. His hair was damp, and he smelled like soap.

"Why don't you come with me to the kitchen?" Jake invited. "We can talk there."

She nodded, sidestepped Hoskins with a smile, then followed Jake into the kitchen. There wasn't a stove, but there was an avocado-colored refrigerator and a micro-wave, as well as two different coffeemakers. He made a beeline for one of them.

"Can I get you some coffee?" he asked.

"Sure." She reached for the plastic container on the counter, helping herself to a packet of creamer and way too many sugars. She liked her coffee embarrassingly sweet.

His eyes met hers over the cup he handed her, his shadowed and haggard gaze far removed from the guy who'd laughingly teased her about eating a calzone the size of her head. "What brings you here?" He sounded bewildered, but not unhappy to see her.

"I heard what happened," she said simply. "Through the newspaper office."

"So you're here on business?"

"No, nothing like that! I was…worried about you."

His face went completely blank, then a slow, lopsided smile emerged. "Worried about me, huh?" His soft laugh made her feel a bit inane, the way she had in the parking lot when she'd wondered if this was a good idea.

"That's funny?" she asked, more defensively than she'd intended.

"No, not at all." His quick denial soothed her misgivings. "It's a novelty. I'm…"

"More used to taking care of others than having them worry about you?" She knew from experience how protective he could be of Giff.

He sat at one of the two card tables in the unadorned room and gestured for her to join him. "Some of my earliest memories are of worrying about my dad, who'd been shot. Then worrying about my mom because she cried a lot. And worrying in general because Dad yelled so much. Wasn't much I could for either of them."

"And now you're in a profession where you spend all your time trying to save people." Didn't take Freud to figure out how *that* had happened. Of course, if that little girl today pulled through, her parents were going to be forever grateful that Jake McBride had happened along.

"It's not like we're jumping into burning buildings on an hourly basis," he said. "Most of what we do is community service stuff, like teaching first-aid certification and giving fire prevention and safety lectures to local… schools." His voice broke just a fraction, and she ached for him.

He stared past Brooke, unseeing, no doubt reliving

the accident scene. "She looked so small. And broken. She was discolored, not breathing. I've called over to the hospital. They're having to delay several of the surgeries she needs because they're not sure she can, that she's strong enough. It's a catch twenty-two. Her body doesn't have a shot at healing without the operations, but they can't operate until she's healed some."

Brooke bit her lip, wondering if there was anything she could say right now that wasn't a trite platitude. Finally she settled on, "She's alive. And she has a chance." *Thanks to you*.

His fingers clenched on his coffee cup, but he nodded in agreement. "I'll check with the hospital again tomorrow."

"You're working tonight?" Maybe that would be better than his being home alone.

Another nod. "My shift doesn't end until tomorrow night. But I'll be at your and Giff's party. I switched a shift with someone else."

She'd completely forgotten about the party. And her parents' latest fight and everything else but checking on Jake. Even though there wasn't a damn thing she could actually do to help him or that girl. *I should go*. But she wouldn't be stopping by Meg's as planned. In light of other people's real tragedies, she didn't have the patience to listen to her mom sniff about how Everett tried to dictate her spending habits while *he* thought nothing of dropping a hundred dollars on a risotto pan or owning two different dessert torches even though he'd never once made the promised crème brûlée.

She reached into her purse, pulling out a business

card and a pen. "I guess I'll see you Friday, then. In the meantime... Here. That's my cell number. In case you ever want to talk," she said lamely.

He took the card, his expression bemused.

"So." She stood. "Bye?"

"You want me to walk you out?" he offered.

"Nah." She smiled. "I can find my way." With a little finger wave, she headed for the door.

"Brooke?" He didn't turn to face her. Was his expression as strained with emotion as his voice? "Thank you."

Chapter Nine

"That's what you're wearing?" Brooke asked from the edge of Meg's queen-size waterbed, a piece of furniture that ate up nearly all of the square footage in the room.

Almost immediately, Brooke regretted any hint of censure in her tone—Meg had proven supportive and surprisingly reliable in all wedding planning so far—but her sister was bound to cause a stir in the orange halter dress. *How does she manage that much cleavage when she's actually a smaller cup size than me?* And then there was the short skirt which gave the illusion that diminutive Meg had mile-long legs.

Her sister paused in the act of applying dark lipstick, raising an eyebrow in the vanity mirror. "I happen to think I look nice."

"You do. You look great," Brooke admitted. At a beach party the festive little number would have been perfect. But for Brooke's future relatives and members of some of Houston's most exclusive country clubs?

Meg sighed. "No offense, baby sister, but I'm not sure I want fashion advice from a woman who looks like she's going to deliver a eulogy at the funeral of some congressman."

"Hey, the little black dress is a classic," Brooke protested.

The door to the master bathroom—technically the *only* bathroom in Meg's one bedroom apartment—swung open and Didi emerged with a trilled "Ready!" In her ruffled yellow dress, she looked like some sort of exotic bird as she flitted toward her daughters. "Meg, darling, you look striking."

"Thank you," Meg said pointedly.

Brooke, knowing she was outnumbered, excused herself with a mumbled, "Think I'll go get a soft drink."

Since Didi had been sleeping on the sleeper sofa for the past couple of days, Brooke had to step over her mother's duffel bags to make her way to the tiny kitchen. Meg had made such eccentric decorating choices that guests were distracted from their impending claustrophobia. Deliberately mismatched appliances somehow went together with the retro covers of old cooking magazines Meg had collected at garage sales and Traders Village, Houston's gigantic indoor flea market. It was funny how Meg's cheap, ramshackle efficiency apartment, located in a neighborhood that barely qualified as safe, evidenced far more personality and care than Brooke's nicer, cleaner place near the mall.

Frowning, Brooke poured herself a diet soda. *I have personality, too. I'm just not emotionally attached to my apartment. I'll decorate when I move in with Giff.* Of course, his house was so perfectly appointed that she couldn't think of a thing she would change. For some reason, that thought depressed her.

Snap out of it. So her fiancé had good taste—how was that a problem?

Meg and Didi appeared, all finished with last-minute hair checks and cosmetic applications, and Brooke stepped outside, vowing to leave behind her irrational melancholy. The Nichols women had decided that, rather than taking multiple cars to the same location, they'd drive into the city together. She could make sure no one got lost on the way to Grace's, and Brooke would be on hand to facilitate introductions between her mom, sister and future mother-in-law.

Her father was teaching a private cooking class and had promised to meet them there no later than twenty minutes after the party had started. As far as Brooke knew, her parents hadn't spoken to each other since Didi had moved in with Meg. Brooke wasn't sure how they would react to each other tonight, but she sent up a silent prayer that the evening would go smoothly.

Houston traffic was the usual nightmare, and Brooke was grateful for the company during the drive. Meg had downloaded some MP3s from new bands she thought Brooke might like. As soon as they'd heard enough of each song to figure out the chorus, all three of them sang along with gusto. Didi, who'd revisited her goal of being a performance artist and had taken voice lessons in the nineties, was particularly good.

A fact that she herself was not shy about acknowledging. "The pipes are still in killer shape, eh? Brooke, I could sing at your wedding! Add a little more razzle-dazzle to the ceremony."

Meg must have noticed the way her sister clenched the steering wheel because she gently redirected the topic. "I've been meaning to ask about the songs you and Giff are using. Knowing you, music was the first thing you decided."

"Actually, no. Finding the dress and getting the invitations out were more time sensitive," Brooke said, happy to have those chores behind her. "We haven't pinned down all the musical selections yet. Oh, shoot—I think I was supposed to turn there."

Talk of wedding plans was temporarily suspended as Brooke navigated several wealthy neighborhoods. Her mother made approving noises, saying that she was glad Brooke was marrying someone who could provide so well for her.

"*You'll* never have to give a detailed defense every time you decide to buy a skirt and matching earrings," Didi muttered sourly.

Meg, on the other hand, shuddered at their opulent surroundings. "All the perfectly manicured matching lawns and three-door garages? It seems too sterile. I mean, to each her own. If you *want* a Stepford life—"

"Meg, do me a favor and don't share that opinion with anyone at the party tonight? Stick to 'thanks for having us' and 'lovely home, Mrs. Baker.' Although, naturally, she'll ask you to call her Grace. Trust me, she's not at all cold or Stepford. She's a terrific woman. And it was darling of her to throw us this party."

This elicited a dramatic sniffle from the backseat. "It

should be your father and I throwing this celebration! I wish we could help more with all of the wedding costs. You *know* that I never wanted you and your sister to do without. I have firsthand experience—"

"Mom." Brooke threw herself in front of the pity train, hoping to derail it before it picked up steam. "Meg and I are doing just fine. We're hardly impoverished waifs. And Giff and I are employed adults in our thirties. We have no problem paying for our own wedding."

When Brooke handed her car keys over to one of the valets Grace had hired for the night, she thought it might spur more comments from her mother about money or the lack thereof, but Didi was staring ahead at the three-story house.

"Do you think your father's already here?" The frosty edge in her tone didn't completely mask the wistfulness beneath it.

"Doubt it," Brooke said. "You know he had that class tonight. He'll be along as soon as he can. Mom, I know the two of you have had some differences this week, but you will put that aside for tonight, won't you?"

Didi froze at the front door, flashing a wounded look at her daughter. "Are you worried that I'm going to embarrass you? Is that how you see your own mother, as an *embarrassment?*"

The open bar was sounding better and better.

Thankfully Brooke was spared answering—she couldn't think of anything that was both tactful and honest—because Grace had opened the door.

"Brooke!" Grace was a combination of girlish enthusiasm and dignified elegance in her royal blue dress and pearls. "And this must be your sister and mother, although, goodness gracious, all three of you could be mistaken for sisters, couldn't you?"

Didi beamed. "Didi Nichols, pleased to meet you. You've raised a wonderful son."

Grace hugged each of them and ushered them into a high-ceilinged foyer furnished with a grandfather clock, antique side table and several decorative mirrors.

"The caterers and band are all set up in the back-yard," Grace said, "but Giff's in the study."

She indicated the spacious room to her left, and Brooke saw Giff pouring Scotch for a business contact Brooke vaguely recognized, a tall man Grace identified as a second cousin and Jake McBride.

Meg's gaze zeroed in on Jake. Out of the corner of her mouth, she whispered, *"Whoa. Who is that?"*

"He's the best man."

"I'll say!"

"If I go in there and introduce the two of you, do you promise to behave?"

Meg was already headed for the foursome of well-dressed men, moving with admirable grace in her stiletto heels. "Not even a little."

Since Grace had just offered to give Didi a tour of the house, Brooke hurried after her sister. After all, this was Brooke's engagement party and she'd yet to greet her fiancé.

Jake spotted her first and smiled warmly. But as his gaze swept over her, his expression changed. He looked puzzled.

Without being too obvious, Brooke did a quick

double-check of her appearance. Did she have a run in her hose, a missing button? She hadn't had anything to eat yet, so she wasn't worried that she had food smudged on her face.

Finding nothing amiss, she gave up wondering why he was nearly frowning at her and said hello to everyone. Giff kissed both her and Meg on the cheeks and took over the introductions.

When Meg shook Jake's hand, she tilted her head to the side, studying him. "Have we met before? There's something familiar about you…"

Jake glanced over her shoulder and winked at Brooke, who couldn't hold back a laugh as she recalled their first meeting at Comida Buena and her instant recognition of him.

"I have some good news," Jake said abruptly, his gaze still tangled with Brooke's. "That little girl? They stabilized her enough to begin her numerous operations, and it looks as if she'll pull through. She has a long road of physical rehab ahead of her, of course, but—"

"That's *wonderful!*" Brooke said, at the same time Giff and Meg both asked, "What little girl?"

As Jake was giving them a brief update on the accident earlier this week, downplaying his role as hero of the day, Brooke noticed that a tuxedoed member of the hired staff had just opened the front door to Everett Nichols.

"There's Dad," she said. "Meg, we should go say hi to him."

Meg didn't look thrilled about tearing herself

away from Jake's side, but she dutifully accompanied Brooke.

"Jake is Mr. July," Brooke said under her breath. "Your fireman calendar? That's where you know him from."

Meg sucked in a breath. "You're close personal friends with one of the hunks from that calendar and never bothered to mention it? Or introduce me!"

"You met some of his colleagues and deemed them hunky, too, as I recall. How many hot guys do you need to know?" What Brooke had meant as a joke came out almost waspish. Was she suddenly feeling *possessive* of Jake?

Ridiculous.

"Little sister," Meg said as they reached the foyer, "a woman can never know too many hot guys."

"Well, sorry I forgot to mention it before now. I've had other things on my mind." *Case in point.* Brooke smiled in welcome. "Hi, Daddy."

Everett beamed at them. "If it isn't the two most beautiful young ladies in Texas."

Meg laughed. "Not that young."

"Speak for yourself," Brooke protested. "Can we get you something to drink, Dad?"

"The person who let me in is bringing me back a beer."

"That sounds good. I think I'll go see about one of those, too." Meg disappeared down the hall in the direction of the backyard. The live band hadn't started playing yet, but it sounded as if they were running a final sound check.

"You must've made great time," Brooke told her father. "I wasn't expecting you for another fifteen or twenty minutes."

"I dismissed class a few minutes early. I wanted you to know how important you are to me. Plus, I wanted to make a good first impression on your future mother-in-law," he added with a grin.

"I appreciate that. Grace will be back down soon. She's showing Mom the house."

Everett's jaw tightened.

"Dad? Everything all right?"

"Other than your mother being pathologically unable to handle any constructive criticism and running off in a tantrum instead of owning up to her mistakes, everything is right as rain."

Brooke stifled a groan. "Dad, I know you and Mom are in the midst of a disagreement right now, but tonight is very—"

"Oh, you don't have to worry about me making a scene, pumpkin." He ruffled her hair. "*I'm* a mature adult."

Here we go.

"YOU LOOK LIKE YOU COULD USE this," Giff said near her ear.

Brooke turned to a reminder of just how lucky she was—an incredibly handsome man in dark suit, his smile illuminated by overhead twinkle lights, holding out a glass of chilled white wine. What woman wouldn't be delighted by that tableau?

She'd just torn herself away from a few Junior League

ladies. They'd expressed thinly veiled curiosity over why Giff hadn't chosen his prospective bride from among *their* ranks, then issued invitations for Brooke to get involved in local volunteer efforts once she was married. Thinking about what it would be like to spend more time with those women than Kresley, who'd be almost an hour away with traffic, was a little depressing. So she'd been standing on the bottom steps of the deck scanning the crowd for her friend and editor when Giff approached.

"Thank you." She accepted the wine gratefully. Showing great restraint, she opted not to down it like a lush and instead smiled at Giff. "And might I add, nice to see you again, stranger. I feel like we've been pulled in different directions all night."

He nodded. "Dozens of people here wanting to speak to us and offer their congrats. It's demanding work, being the guests of honor."

"Especially when one of us has been busy babysitting her so-called parents," Brooke added darkly.

His expression was sympathetic. "They're still not getting along?"

"No, but at least they're showing the good sense to avoid each other rather than fight." She pointed to Meg and Didi, talking to other guests at one of the tables. Everett, meanwhile, was waltzing with Grace near the bandstand. Brooke smiled impishly. "You know, I have an idea of how you could take my mind off my family woes."

He followed her gaze to the dance floor. "I have been eager to dance with you all night," he lied unabashedly.

"I've just been waiting for the band to play something appropriately romantic."

"By which you mean something so slow that we barely have to move, and you can just put your arms around me and sway?"

He grinned. "You say it like that's a bad thing."

The current song ended and was replaced with a feisty, up-tempo number. Giff winced.

"Don't worry," Brooke said laughingly. "I wouldn't— Uh-oh." Everett had released Grace and was now dancing with someone else, a brunette. An extremely pretty brunette. Across the lawn Didi had shot to her feet, a stormy expression on her face.

Meg stood too, placing a hand on their mother's shoulder. *Thank you, Megan, I take back every single uncharitable thing I ever thought about you.* Relieved that potential disaster had been averted, Brooke turned back to Giff but didn't get a chance to say anything before she was interrupted by Grace.

"Giff, darling, the Petersens are leaving. I thought you might like to see them out?" she suggested. Her smile at Brooke was conspiratorial. "As I'm sure you know, Dermott Petersen is a major shareholder in two large corporations and Giff has been campaigning for their business for several years now."

"Right." Giff started up the steps, then hesitated when he saw Jake coming out of the house. "Perfect timing."

Jake raised his eyebrows in question. "For?"

"Brooke was just saying how much she wanted to dance, but unfortunately, duty calls."

"Unfortunately," Brooke echoed, shooting Giff an amused but pointed look.

"No one ever had to twist my arm to get me to dance with a beautiful woman," Jake said. He held out a hand. "Shall we?"

"I'll be back soon," Giff promised over his shoulder, taking the stairs two at a time.

Jake shook his head. "Work, work, work. Even at his own party."

"He has an admirable work ethic," Brooke said tolerantly. "And a gut-level aversion to the dance floor."

Jake laughed with her as they cut through the crowd. She experienced an odd jolt when he put a hand on her waist—this wasn't like the freestyle club dancing they'd done at the concert. This was actual hold-your-partner-in-your-arms contact, and it made her pulse a little fluttery.

Trying to mask her sudden shyness over their proximity, she stared up at him. "You look good. B-better, I mean. Than when I saw you the other day. I'm so glad to hear that little girl's prognosis has improved."

Jake nodded, his eyes somber for a second, before brightening. "You look good, too. Different but good."

"Different?" Exhilaration pulsed through her when he spun her out in a quick circle.

"Darker," he clarified with a glance down at her black cocktail dress. "I've seen you in vivid yellow, red and that pink sweater you were wearing the other day at the station."

Brooke chuckled. "You hadn't struck me as a guy who paid so much attention to women's clothes."

"I'm not."

Unsure how to respond, she was relieved when he began speaking again instead of letting them lapse into an awkward silence.

"You look great tonight," he said. "I was trying, somewhere in there, to pay you a compliment. I guess I'm just more used to seeing you as bright and colorful."

That caught her so unawares she accidentally squashed his toes beneath her feet. Bright and colorful? *Me?* She'd grown up feeling staid, if not downright stuffy, compared to the rest of her family. The only person who'd ever called her "bright" had been a college professor who'd been referring solely to her academic potential.

"Brooke?"

"Sorry. You just surprised me. You have a knack for that," she added wryly.

"Oh." He hesitated. "That's not a good thing, is it? As I recall, you hate surprises."

She bit her lip. "I'm discovering that I like some more than others."

Their gazes met, and she was struck anew by how gorgeous his eyes were. Was it inappropriate to notice that? She quickly glanced away, looking past his shoulder.

"Hey!" Relief bubbled up within her. "There's Kres."

Kresley and Dane Flynn were only a few feet away on the dance floor, moving slower than the beat but both smiling.

"A friend, I take it?"

Brooke nodded. "Good friend. Also my editor. I was

looking for her just before Giff and I ran into you." This gave her an excellent excuse to extricate herself from Jake's embrace. Despite how much she'd enjoyed dancing with him— Well, that was the problem, wasn't it? How much she'd enjoyed dancing with him.

She pulled away abruptly. "Kresley!"

The Flynns waved and left the dance floor, meeting up with her along the side. Kresley was gorgeous tonight in a deep green maternity dress; standing next to her, Brooke recalled Jake's words and wondered if perhaps she did look a bit drab. Tonight she was supposed to *celebrating*. Maybe something more festive—

"You must be Jake?" Kresley tilted her head, regarding him with a puckish smile. "Kresley Flynn. I've heard a lot about you."

Brooke shot Kresley a warning glance that didn't entirely match her friendly tone. "Kres, Dane, this is Jake McBride, Giff's friend and our best man."

"Nice to meet you." As he was shaking hands with both of them, Brooke heard her name being called.

Meg was barreling down on them. "Brooke! Hey, Kresley, Dane." She paused, her voice becoming a purr. "Jake. I don't mean to interrupt, but can I borrow my sister for a moment?"

"I'll be right back," Brooke said, hoping that was true and whatever emergency Meg was telegraphing with her eyes would be quickly settled. "Will you guys let Giff know, in case he comes looking for me?"

She barely waited for their nods before trailing Meg toward the house and up the deck stairs.

"Mom's in meltdown mode," Meg said. "I took her

glass of Riesling away and suggested she go inside to freshen up."

If they hadn't arrived together—a decision Brooke was seriously rethinking in retrospect—she might suggest that Meg take their mother home. Or, if Didi and Everett would act like adults who hadn't spent Brooke's entire life creating drama, *they* could go home together.

The sniffling coming from behind the closed door let Brooke know which first-floor guest bathroom her mother occupied. She took a deep breath and knocked. "Mom?"

Didi opened the door and peered out with reddened eyes. Streaks of mascara were beginning to smudge the tops of her cheeks. "It's a l-lovely party, Brooke. And Grace is every bit as wonderful as you've described her."

Brooke sighed. "You don't look like you're having a 'lovely' time. Maybe you and Dad just need to talk, then you'll feel better. I could go find him. You two could go home and—"

"Oh, I wouldn't *dream* of ruining your father's fun," Didi said tightly. "Haven't you seen him out there, flirting up women half his age? After I gave him the best years of my life! Do you know how hard it is for a middle-aged woman to start over again?"

Throughout their youth, Meg and Brooke had been warned multiple times that their parents might be separating. Should Brooke actually worry that this time there might be a grain of truth in the sentiment? *Figures. They split up the night of my engagement party. Maybe they can find a way to get divorce papers served during my wedding.*

Brooke was instantly appalled at herself. Was she really becoming so cynical?

"Mom, I love you. You know I do. But—"

"But I'm being a dark cloud, aren't I? Everyone is so happy for you and Giff. The guests have been talking about what a cute couple you are all night. People told me how pretty the wedding invitations were, and it made me realize—I never had any of that, the fuss, the big day. Maybe I shouldn't be surprised that Everett and I have had so many problems. He never even thought I was worth all that effort. Our wedding was so…expedient."

"Is it possible your mood is coloring your memory of the event? You've always told me how passionate and romantic it was to be caught up in the moment," Brooke pointed out.

"Yes, well." Didi gave her a bitter little smile. "I guess we should just be glad you learned from my mistakes and won't let yourself get caught up in romance."

Brooke blinked. *She has a point.* But what did it say about a bride-to-be who, at her own engagement party, was feeling grateful not to succumb to romance?

Chapter Ten

Brooke found Giff at the bottom of the steps in the backyard and flashed him a wan smile. "We have to stop meeting like this."

He took her hand. "I was just coming to find you. Thought maybe you'd been kicking up your heels on the dance floor this whole time."

"No, but it looks like Jake and the Flynns are still over in that area. We should visit with them before Kresley gets tired and has to bail. Actually, I might not be able to stay too much later myself. Meg and I probably need to take Mom home." She tried to keep the weariness out of her voice, but could tell by the gentle concern in Giff's expression that she hadn't succeeded.

"I'm so sorry your parents are arguing," he told her. "It must be difficult for you. But I'm sure they'll have everything smoothed over soon."

"You're probably right." Brooke bit her lip. "To hear Mom tell it, this fight is the big one, but then, that's how she always sees them. Thank God we'll never have to worry about this kind of angst and drama in our marriage! You're so...*stable*."

"Wow. I sound very dashing," he said wryly.

Her cheeks flushed. "Sorry. I meant it as high praise."

"Brooke, you're back!" Kresley had kicked off her shoes and was sitting at a table with her husband and Jake. "Jake was just telling us about how he got inspired to do his road trips."

Taking a seat, Brooke glanced questioningly at Jake. He'd claimed before that he liked to go wherever the spirit moved him—she hadn't known there was a specific inspiration behind it.

"When I was in the Middle East, I met a kid from Kentucky," Jake explained for Brooke's benefit. "He was from a town of about three hundred, had never been away from home before and was scared. Told me once that it would be ironic if he died for his country because he'd never *seen* any of it. We both made it back in one piece, and once I got home to Texas, I realized I was a lot like him.

"I've lived my entire life here, and while I'm in no rush to change that, I do want to visit all fifty states, make an effort to see the country I served. My next trip is to Tennessee. I have four consecutive days off starting Thursday, and a buddy of mine is flying me to Chattanooga. There's a tourist spot there where you're supposed to be able to see seven different states."

"He's already been to Alaska," Kresley told Brooke.

"The military made that part easy," he interjected. "I was on a base there for six months."

"And he plans to go to Hawaii soon," Kresley added.

"With those two out of the way, the other forty-eight seem comparatively simple."

Jake laughed. "Comparatively. People forget just how big this country is."

"They do," Kresley said, sitting straighter in her chair. "Thanks to Twitter and Facebook, you can know exactly what people a thousand miles away are doing every minute. You know, I think this would make an excellent human-interest piece for the lifestyles section! Local man, a community hero, no less—"

"Oh, boy, she's on a roll now," Dane said affectionately.

Ignoring her husband's interjection, Kresley continued, "A former soldier, trying to get to know America."

Jake's eyes widened and he fidgeted uncomfortably, eliciting a laugh from Brooke. The man willingly walked into infernos but seemed nervous about having a story done on him.

He scowled in her direction. "You think it's silly, don't you? An article about me?"

"Not at all," she hastily clarified. "I was laughing at… something else. I think the story could turn out really well."

Giff was nodding his agreement. "Maybe you could even write it, Brooke. You're always saying you love the opportunities to do more than weddings."

Jake raised an eyebrow. "The woman about to get married doesn't like weddings?"

"I like weddings just fine," she grumbled, trying to

ignore her earlier misgivings that she should be more excited about all of this. More *bridal,* somehow.

"Then it's settled," Kresley said in the authoritative tone Brooke recognized from countless staff meetings. "I'll have to look at the budget before we nail down travel specifics, but Jake, you said a friend was flying you to Tennessee?"

"He's a flight instructor, owns a Cessna Skyhawk."

"What do you think he might charge for Brooke to go with you?" Kresley asked.

Brooke whipped her head around. "What?"

"As long as Jake doesn't mind the extra company, I can approve Thursday and Friday out of the office and look into the budget for a hotel room." Kresley shrugged. "It's for work, but you'll need to take your own pictures. I am not sending a photographer, too."

That was no big deal—there were several staffers, Brooke included, who'd done double duty at the *Chronicle* before, getting the byline for both story and photos. Being sent away overnight with Jake McBride, however, seemed like a huge, towering, everything's-bigger-in-Texas deal.

Brooke glanced at Giff. "You wouldn't have a problem with this?"

He looked surprised by the question. "It would be silly for me to object—*I'm* the one who suggested you write it. Besides, it gives me that much more time to work around the clock guilt-free so I can clear my schedule for after the wedding."

They planned to honeymoon in Puerto Vallarta,

Mexico, and also take a few days to get her moved into his house.

The thought of their honeymoon caused a strange twist in Brooke's stomach—*maybe it's anticipation*—and she turned to Jake. "We haven't really confirmed that you're okay with this. I—"

"Sure," he said, surprising her with his easy agreement. He'd seemed less than enthusiastic when Kresley first proposed the article. "I don't know that people really want to read about me, but if you and Kresley think so, then I'm happy to help. We can always kill time on the way up there swapping embarrassing stories about Giff."

Brooke's fiancé groaned good-naturedly. "Is it too late to change my answer?"

"Last I heard," Jake told Kresley, "my buddy's planning to drop me and one paying customer. A Skyhawk seats three in addition to the pilot. I'll check with him and see if the space is still available. Since Brooke's with me, I doubt Boom would charge more than a nominal fee, if that."

"Boom?" Brooke echoed. He wanted her to put her livelihood and well-being in the hands of a grown man who answered to *Boom?* Wasn't that the sound a plane made when it freaking crashed?

"When you say 'drop,'" Brooke began, "you are just being colloquial, right? Before I even consider going, you have to promise there would be no parachutes involved."

Amid chuckles around the table, Jake said, "No,

he'll land the plane. There will be an actual runway and everything."

"Good." Because being around Jake already felt too much like a freefall.

JAKE GLANCED UP AT THE STARS, not that he could actually see any from the Grace's backyard. That was one thing money couldn't buy. The house was stunning, if you weren't overwhelmed by three stories and the one or two formal rooms that looked like something from a magazine layout, but the night sky was largely blotted out by city lights and smog. Jake's own modest home outside Houston and beyond Sugar Land didn't have four bathrooms, but most nights he could find a half-dozen constellations without trouble.

After the live music that had been playing for the past three hours and the spirited conversations of guests, the yard was subdued now, with only the clatter of caterers packing up to compete with the sound of crickets. He'd made the offer to stick around and help clean, but since Grace was already paying other people to do that, there wasn't much to be done.

Still she'd thanked him for the effort. "Such a good boy. Your mother must be so proud," she'd added shrewdly.

He'd managed not to wince in guilt, but her seemingly innocent comment had hit home. He knew he should visit his parents, talk to them more at the very least. They'd been invited tonight, but by the time the party had been announced, Mrs. McBride had already made travel plans to go help her favorite aunt after a double knee replacement. It had been implied that Mr. McBride wasn't comfortable going solo to an event where there was an open bar, and Jake couldn't bring himself to volunteer as the old man's party parole officer.

Jake wanted to believe his mom's optimism that his father would make it to—and beyond—his upcoming one-year anniversary of sobriety without slipping up, but it sounded too much like the false promises Jake had heard when he was younger. Even after long stretches of success, his dad had fallen off the wagon every time, each backslide more painful because of the hopeful months that had preceded it.

Giff had said that since Jake wasn't in a hurry to leave, he should stick around and have a beer; it felt like they'd only seen each other in passing during the party. But given his bitter reminiscing about booze, Jake went inside and stopped his friend before Giff reached the refrigerator.

"On second thought, make mine a soft drink," Jake said.

"Good thinking. It's been a long night and we each still have to drive home."

"Is your mom going to come down and join us?" No sooner had Jake finished his sentence than pipes above him creaked to life, the sound of a shower or bath being run upstairs.

"No," Giff said with his head inside the fridge. "I told her I'd stick around until they're finished outside and lock up for her. She's beat. But happy! Did you see what a good time she was having tonight? She looked like herself again. It's nice to see her laughing, socializing."

Giff straightened and shut the door, then carried two bottled sodas from the fridge and brought them toward the oval kitchen table. Déjà vu struck Jake with the force of a blow.

How many times as a kid had he sat at this exact polished wooden surface, waiting for Giff to bring over drinks or snacks? He could almost smell Grace's home-made brownies baking in the oven. In fourth grade, they'd done their math homework here. A few years later, they'd been making bets in the sun-filled kitchen on who could get a date first to the middle school Valentine's Day dance. By high school, Jake was often included in family breakfasts on Saturdays, after staying the night at the Baker house following Friday's football games. He had a vivid memory of Mr. Baker looking at him over Grace's whimsical salt and pepper shakers and pronouncing, "I'm proud of you, son."

The back of Jake's throat burned. He'd thought recently that he'd never experienced that sense of being home—of truly belonging—but that was only half accurate. The Bakers had given him that gift. Except that he wasn't *truly* one of them. At the end of the afternoon or even the end of the weekend, he'd always had to return to his real place. To the house with two bathrooms, neither of which included reliable plumbing, the mother with consistently swollen eyes she liked to pretend he couldn't see and the raging alcoholic of a father.

Jake suddenly saw his shock over Giff's engagement with new clarity. It wasn't just disbelief over how quickly it had happened. He'd been projecting his inability to ever envision *himself* married. Giff, on the other hand, had grown up at this table with parents who adored both him and each other.

Giff and Brooke would no doubt carry on that tradition, with a table of their own in some kitchen where Jake would be invited for birthdays and maybe an occasional Thanksgiving. Ignoring an unexpectedly fierce stab of resentment—*I'm better than that, I* want *him to be happy*—Jake admonished himself to get on board. He was supposed to be Giff's wingman, to support him no matter what. The engagement wasn't Jake's decision to second-guess, and he needed to stop busting Giff's chops.

Which was why he hated himself a little for saying, "You know who I was thinking about?"

"Give me a hint."

"Veronica Dean."

Giff let out a low whistle.

"Exactly."

Both men had met Veronica right after high school graduation, but Jake had paused to wonder if he was good enough for her. Suffering no such compunction, Giff had asked her out first and the two of them had been hot and heavy until he left for College Station in the fall, after which their relationship had trailed to a natural conclusion.

Jake gestured with his bottle. "You were gaga over that woman. I remember the way you used to look at her."

Giff grinned boyishly, momentarily channeling his eighteen-year-old self. "Can you blame me? It was *Veronica Dean*."

"You don't look at Brooke like that." Saying it out loud felt like the worst kind of betrayal, but the resulting guilt didn't make the words any less true.

"Dammit, Jake!" Giff slammed his bottle down on the table. The carbonated beverage immediately began to bubble and fizz up over the plastic. "I can't believe this. I thought you finally liked Brooke—"

"I do."

"—and now you ambush me with…what? The fact that I've *matured* since I was a horny teenager?"

"That wasn't my—"

"If you're looking for a way to suggest Brooke isn't good enough for me, you should probably leave now."

"That's not at all what I meant," Jake said in a low voice. The truth was that he'd heard Giff rhapsodize more about his mother's joy in the engagement than Brooke's. While Brooke and Giff seemed perfectly fond of each other, there was no evidence of more than that.

"Good. You're going to have to accept Brooke." Giff, looking ticked off but slightly less murderous, ran a hand through his hair. "Because this whole question of whether she deserves to marry into the 'fabulous Baker' family is ridiculous. That's *your* issue, pal, not mine."

Jake kept his mouth shut. Saying anything else would be as futile and potentially dangerous as throwing water on an electrical fire. Besides, there was no diplomatic way to explain that this was not a question of whether Brooke was deserving.

It was about *her* deserving *more*.

Chapter Eleven

"Explain this to me again." Meg, who wasn't working since it was Wednesday night, wiggled over on Brooke's bed to make room for the open suitcase. "I'm the vivacious one who, let's face it, puts out, yet you are somehow the one who is engaged to the rich guy *and* going away for the weekend with his hot friend? There are so many things wrong with that I don't know where to begin."

Brooke glared. "I am not 'going away for the weekend' with Jake. All right, technically, yes. I am. But not the way you insinuated."

"Uh-huh." Whether she was convinced or not, Meg had the good sense to change the subject. "Have you ever flown on one of these puddle jumpers before? It won't exactly be the first-class section." As if either of them had ever flown first-class.

"I'm aware." Did private planes come with strategically placed air-sickness bags the same way commercial flights did? Squelching the unpleasant thought, Brooke narrowed her eyes. "Remind me why you're here, with your oh-so-helpful observations, instead of back at your place."

"After a week of Mom's company, my place seems lonely now that she's gone."

Meg had reported yesterday morning that, fed up with their mother's rants about Everett's hypothetical affairs, she'd finally offered to tail him, as if Didi were a real client who suspected her spouse of cheating. Instead of taking Meg's offer, Didi had seemed terrified that her daughter might find something and had quickly fled home to make peace with her husband. Brooke didn't for a moment think that her dad would really be unfaithful, but his blatant flirting whenever he and his wife fought wasn't exactly the moral high ground, either.

"I haven't heard from her since she left," Meg said. "You don't think they've finally killed each other, do you?"

Brooke paused in the act of folding a pair of jeans, considering. "Nah. I work in the news industry. We would have broken the story of a double homicide by now."

"Because the *Katy Chronicle* is such a cutting-edge paper." Meg giggled.

"Hey—unnecessary! I have a steady paycheck, a boss I like and free admittance to a number of hoity-toity social events." That was, after all, how she'd met Giff in the first place.

"No offense." Meg held up her hands. "I was just razzing you because I'm your sister and it's what siblings do. The truth is…"

"Yeah?"

"Maybe I envy you. A little. You found your niche."

It was unheard of for Meg to sound so woebegone. Brooke plopped down on the mattress next to her. "You'll find yours, too. This P.I. thing—"

Meg snorted. "I don't think so. It sounded exciting at first—very Sam Spade and retro sexy—but it's a lot of paperwork, computer searches and car stakeouts. Do you know how *dull* a stakeout can be?"

"Not through firsthand experience, no."

"Trust me. You spend half the time trying not to think about how much you have to go to the bathroom and the other half stuffing your face just to keep awake. I'd be a size ten inside a month."

"Heaven forfend."

Overlooking her curvier sister's sarcasm, Meg continued, "Being a P.I. wouldn't be half as interesting as *your* job."

"Writing up weddings?" For a moment, Brooke forgot to defend her venerable position as journalist.

"Admit it, aren't you at least a little bit thrilled to be jetting off with Jake McBride? Focusing entirely on him under the guise of doing a story?"

"Why do I see air quotes when you say that? You do realize I really *am* doing a story, right?" Of course, no story Brooke had ever covered before had left her with a case of butterflies like she had now, not even when she'd interviewed the governor of Texas while she was still a college student in Austin. Every time she thought about her trip to Tennessee with Jake, she simultaneously wanted to grin and throw up.

The nausea is not nerves over being alone with the man. It's probably just anxiety because of the puddle jumper. Piloted by the inauspiciously named Boom, *for pity's sake.* Under those circumstances, who wouldn't want to toss her cookies?

"What is *that?*" Meg frowned at the faded extra-large T-shirt Brooke held. It showed a crazy-eyed stick figure peering over a typewriter and read Hand Over the Caffeine and No One Gets Hurt.

"A nightshirt."

"You're killing me, sis. Don't you own something black and lacy?"

"Megan! This is a business trip, not my honeymoon. I am engaged to Giff," she said firmly.

"Yeah, engaged to be married. You know how many women in your position indulge in one last fling?"

An erotic and wholly inappropriate picture tried to surface in Brooke's mind. She banished it. "That is tacky and deceitful. I would never do that. Especially with Giff's best friend!"

"Mmm-hmm."

"And just what is that supposed to mean?" Brooke was a grown woman. In theory, she knew better than to let her sister bait her.

In theory.

"Well, if things are as platonic between you and Jake as you say—"

"They are!"

"Then why did you dismember me with your eyes every time I smiled at him during your engagement party?"

For a moment, words eluded Brooke. She recalled exactly the kind of smile Meg had flashed at the handsome fireman. And exactly how it had made Brooke feel. Angry. Possessive.

Brooke swallowed and managed to stammer, "You have an overactive imagination."

Shaking her head, Meg stood. "You know what I recall about your toddler years? The stories you started making up as soon as you could talk. Mom always said I had her artistic streak, but you had the imagination. Brooke, if you're telling yourself that you aren't attracted to Jake McBride, you've become an even better storyteller than I remember."

JAKE HAD CONSIDERED CALLING Brooke—or her editor—to try to get out of this trip. He'd realized in the past few days that this was probably a bad idea. On the other hand, he was already on thin ice with Giff, who would no doubt take Jake's cancellation as a sign of hostility toward Brooke. Which couldn't be further from the truth.

Still, now that he was actually here on her doorstep, hand raised to knock, he found himself smiling at the thought of seeing her again. He'd had a lot of fun the night of the concert and had discovered the potential for rare and deep friendship the evening she'd come to check on him at the station. Part of him—the throw-yourself-on-the-grenade idiot part—was looking forward to this weekend.

She answered the door so quickly it was as if she'd been hovering on the other side, waiting for him. Had she been eager to see him, too? His heart sped up at the thought—probably an adrenal response to impending disaster. After all, his pulse also quickened when faced with the possibility of a backdraft or flashover.

"Hi." Her tone was warm and inviting; she seemed like a different woman than the one who'd answered the door for him the night of the concert.

He lifted his chin, gesturing to the lightweight purple jacket she wore. "Color. I like it."

She laughed, but stopped abruptly. "It's my raincoat. The weather forecast called for scattered showers. Do you think it will be safe to fly?"

Knowing how sincerely she meant her question, he tried to keep from smiling. "Boom's flown through enemy airspace while being shot at and always got where he was going in one piece. I don't think the forty percent chance of light showers is going to slow him down."

"Okay, then." She took a deep breath. "If you say it's all right, I'm done worrying. I trust you."

Don't.

If he were a better man, he would have said the word out loud. Didn't he owe her some warning about his growing suspicion that he might try to talk her out of marrying Giff this weekend?

Jake had always had a strong sense of loyalty, an innate code of honor that he followed. Normally that would be enough to keep him from interfering. The problem was that he was becoming more and more confident that Brooke and Giff getting married would be a mistake, that given the chance, they could each find something stronger and more meaningful with other people.

Like you? his conscience sneered. The line between "good intentions" and "selfish bastard" had become amazingly blurred.

Jake tried to summon the mental picture of her and Giff at a kitchen table, surrounded by the undoubtedly cute kids they would have together. Instead, he imagined a tall, scuffed table in a dingy nightclub where Giff sat awkwardly, making a concerted effort to like a loud indie rock band while Brooke told herself that she didn't mind not dancing, that there were more important qualifications in a potential mate.

"Jake? I know I just got through promising that I wouldn't worry, but I take it back. You look troubled. Is something wrong?"

Other than the risk of my sabotaging your engagement? "Not at all."

THE FLIGHT TO Chattanooga was far smoother than Brooke had imagined it would be.

The landing was not.

Brooke had been on roller coasters at the now de-funct AstroWorld that had rattled her less. The older man who'd been seated with Jake and Brooke—Boom's paying customer—had begun snoring five minutes after take off and hadn't seemed at all disturbed by the screeching jolt of touchdown. Brooke had actually had to wake him up to announce their arrival.

Jake, darn his unflappable hide, looked as if he was

trying not to laugh at her as helped her out of the plane. "You doin' okay?"

"Fine, although I've realized…"

"What?"

She gave a quick toss of her head, feeling stupid. "Nothing. Just one of those old 'what I want to be when I grow up' things. It's for the best that it never panned out."

"Tell me you wanted to be an astronaut," Jake said. "You'd be adorable in a NASA helmet."

"Sorry if things got a little bumpy there at the end," Boom told her. It looked as if he might even be a little red-faced about his landing job, but it was difficult to tell with his naturally ruddy complexion. "So, Jake, see you again Saturday afternoon?"

Jake nodded. "We'll be here. Thanks for the lift, buddy."

The two men shook hands, and then Boom smiled at Brooke. "It was especially nice to meet you, ma'am."

She thanked him sincerely—landing aside, she'd just received a free flight. How often did that happen? And she'd truly enjoyed herself. Jake had given her a lot of information about what a typical day for a firefighter involved when he wasn't fighting fires. For instance, last month, they'd done a practice burn at a house that had been sold to the city and was scheduled for demolition; it had been used as an all-day training activity. And while Brooke had known that firefighters routinely spoke to kids, she'd never really thought about the importance of a child seeing a fireman in his full gear, which could be intimidating.

"The thing with kids," he'd told her, "is that when they get scared, they hide. In closets, under beds. The room is filled with dark smoke, which can be terrifying even to an adult, and then here comes this person in boots and heavy gloves with a tank on his back, breathing through a full face mask. The munchkins are thinking Darth Vader, not good guy."

So the firemen would demonstrate what each piece of equipment was used for, then put it on so that at the conclusion of the presentation, students could actually walk up and interact with the suited-up fireman.

"Hopefully none of these children will ever be in a fire, but if they are, they'll know not to hide from us, which increases the number of lives we can save. Another popular demonstration for the little guys is that we have a race to see which firefighter can get into his or her gear the fastest. I currently hold the station record," he'd boasted.

If Meg had been on the plane, she would have made some bold inquiry about how fast Jake could get *out* of whatever he was wearing. Brooke, however, had more restraint. And a fiancé.

After they'd parted ways with Boom, she and Jake rented a car to get them around Chattanooga. He grinned at her while he unlocked the white sedan. "I'm not used to having someone along for the ride. It's kind of nice."

"Thanks. Let's hope you still feel that way on Saturday. Sometimes you have a distinct 'lone wolf' vibe, and Kresley put you on the spot about taking me along." Brooke frowned thoughtfully. "I think it must be hormone-related. She's not usually an impulsive person."

"Lone wolf, huh? Is that the polite term for antisocial?" Jake teased. "Trust me, I'm plenty used to having to share close quarters with others, and I get along with just about anyone if I need to."

Brooke buckled her seat belt and turned to him expectantly. "So, what's the plan from here?"

"Plan?" He sniffed with overacted derision. "You're missing the point, Ms. Nichols. This isn't an op or a three-alarm. We don't have to follow any plans. We can do whatever we want or do nothing at all, eat dessert before dinner. Wear mismatched socks!"

She pursed her lips, well aware that he was picking on her but amused despite herself. Not that she planned to admit that. "Are you quite finished?"

"Probably not," he said unrepentantly. "Expect random bouts of mockery."

"You and Giff are so different."

Jake slanted her a glance as he started the car. "Meaning he's a gentleman who would never heckle a lady, whereas I'm a cad who doesn't take anything seriously?"

"No. Well, yes," she amended, returning some of the hell he'd been merrily giving her. "But it's more than that. I know the two of you grew up together, which probably accounts for how close you are. Do you think if you'd met say, in high school or college that you would have become such friends?"

He was quiet for a long moment, his expression unexpectedly serious. "I don't know. I hope so. He's a hell of a guy, and probably a good influence on me. Without his family caring about me, I think I easily *could* have become an antisocial lone wolf. I was…angry a lot as a kid."

From what he'd told her about his father's drinking, he'd probably had good reason to be. "I'm glad the Bakers were there for you," she said.

"Yeah. Me, too." His tone was sincere, but the set of his jaw made the proclamation more grim than grateful.

Since Giff was the common denominator between them, it seemed paradoxical that bringing him up had turned a playful conversation tense. Brooke sat quietly in her seat, regretting the strain she'd inadvertently created and not wanting to say anything to make it worse.

As he turned out of the parking lot, Jake broke the silence, his tone casual. "I don't usually go for touristy destinations—sometimes I just go camping somewhere or look for obscure places other people might not know about. But there's actually a lot of popular stuff around Chattanooga I intend to see. The aquarium, the Ruby Falls cavern. Thought we'd drive toward the city, find a hotel and go from there. You have anything particular you want to do while we're here?"

"Thanks for asking, but this is your getaway. I'm just here to document it." If it had been her vacation, she would have preferred the security of knowing they had hotel rooms reserved, but Jake had scoffed that playing it by ear was part of the fun. She took a small tape recorder out of her purse. "You have any objection to being recorded? If I try to take notes in a moving vehicle, I won't be able to read them later. My handwriting is atrocious as is."

Jake did a double take, his head swiveling toward her for a moment before he looked back to the road. "You're kidding."

"Nope. Penmanship was the only bad grade I ever worried about getting in elementary school. With a lot of concentrated effort, I can now manage a decent cursive for a few lines, but I used to write stories when I was a kid. The ideas would come to me so fast, I'd dash everything down while it was fresh in my mind. The only people who could ever read it were my mom and me. Meg teased that it was why she never bothered trying to peek at my diary." Brooke had figured the real reason Meg never bothered to steal a glance was because there was nothing in Brooke's paltry entries that was half as exciting as Meg's real life.

"I can't imagine anything messy about you," Jake said. "Not even handwriting."

"Now you know my shameful secret, the dark truth people on my Christmas card list have only guessed at. I type and print a letter each year. All I handwrite is my name," she admitted.

"Don't tell me you're one of those people who dutifully recaps the year's milestones and has all your cards in the mail right after Thanksgiving?"

"Guilty."

He shot her a smug smile. "Well, when I get the card from you and Giff next December, I won't be fooled."

She thought ahead to Christmas, picturing a beautifully decorated tree, Giff carving the ham, Grace bringing presents wrapped in color-coordinated paper. Yuletide perfection. She smiled to herself, the positive image making her serene.

When she'd been younger—upset that her parents might actually be on the brink of divorce this time or embarrassed that her friends had seen Didi at the local grocery store in makeup and clothes better suited to her showgirl aspirations than the produce aisle—Brooke had retreated to her storybook world. Mothers there did not wear sequined tank tops to PTA meetings and dads yelled only at football teams, not hapless sous-chefs who left the kitchen in tears. The more Brooke visited that alternate reality, the clearer her daydreams had become. And now, like a self-fulfilling prophecy, they were all about to come true.

She was smiling to herself, thinking ahead to what she might get Giff for Christmas when Jake cleared his throat and jolted her back to the present.

"Did I lose you?" Jake asked.

"I…yeah, I guess. My mind wandered. Pretty unprofessional, huh? So, no problem being recorded then?"

"Nope. Fire away."

"Okay. When you got back to the States and realized you wanted to start this road-tripping project, where was the first place you went?"

They chatted easily for the next fifteen minutes as he followed the signs directing them toward the heart of Chattanooga. Finally he interrupted to point out a sign for a franchise hotel.

"What do you think?"

It seemed like one of their better shots at reasonable pricing without being skeevy. "Sure."

Moments later, they were parking in the hotel lot. He held the door for her as they entered the lobby.

The pretty redhead at the check-in counter gave Jake an appraising glance that Brooke tried not to notice. It wasn't as if she had the right to be jealous. *Still.* For all the woman knew, Brooke and Jake were a couple, which made her overly flirtatious smile a tad annoying.

But the woman's smile faded to an apologetic frown after Jake had asked if there were any rooms available.

"No, sorry. Ya'll don't have a reservation? With the big gospel competition this weekend, choirs are comin' in from all over the country. We're booked solid. Most places are gonna be," she added.

Sure enough, Jake and Brooke heard that same prediction at the second and third hotels they tried.

The bald man at the front desk suggested, "You could always try Bob and Erma's up the road."

"Bob and Erma's?" Brooke repeated. "Is that like a local, family-owned motel?"

"No, ma'am. Bob and Erma are empty nesters. All three of their boys went off on basketball scholarships, so they've got rooms to rent."

Stay in a teenager's bedroom while he was away at college? Brooke had a picture of herself sleeping in a room that smelled faintly of gym socks and had posters of bikini-clad models on the wall.

"Uh…thanks for the advice," Jake said, already drawing Brooke toward the door as he added over his shoulder, "We'll keep Bob and Erma in mind as a backup."

Brooke smirked at him as he climbed into the car. "See, *this* is why some of us uptight folks like to plan ahead."

Instead of acknowledging that she had a point, he chided, "Where's your sense of adventure?"

She snorted. "As I believe I've mentioned, everyone else in my family had that part covered. I thought someone might want to give being sensible a shot. For a couple of years, I even tried to bring them around to my way of thinking, but it was like beating my head against a brick wall."

He studied her for a long moment rather than turn the key in the ignition.

She began to feel self-conscious. "What?"

"Nothing, really. Just, I've been there myself. In fifth grade, sixth grade, maybe even as late as seventh, I tried everything I could think of to get my dad to sober up. I ran away once and left a note that I'd be back when he'd gone twenty-four hours without drinking."

Brooke's breath caught. "What happened?"

"He was passed out and never even saw the note. The Bakers made me call my mom, so that she at least knew where I was and that I was safe, and she talked me into coming home. She didn't come right out and say it, but I think she might have been afraid of what my father would do if he got angry enough."

Brooke's heart broke for that long-ago boy; no kid should feel burdened with such adult responsibility.

"You can't help an addict who won't help themselves,"

Jake concluded. "I gave up on him. By the time I was in eighth grade, I'd redirected my efforts from trying to change my dad to trying to get my mother to leave him. She and I could have had a chance at a happy, normal life."

Did he realize that even now, so many years later, he sounded wistful?

Jake shook his head. "But she was as stubborn as the old man, a brick wall in her own passive way. Kept insisting that the man she'd married, the man he'd been before he was shot, was still in there and that she couldn't leave him after all he'd endured. Even if he *has* stopped drinking now," Jake allowed, his tone heavy with doubt, "I can't imagine that all the years she stayed were worth it."

Brooke hesitated. "I noticed that they were on Grace's guest list for the party." They hadn't been invited to the wedding itself simply because it would be so small, mostly family with a few exceptions like Jake and Kresley.

"I know. Mom's out of town, and Dad decided not to come without her."

"When she gets back into town, are you planning on seeing them?" Brooke didn't know the McBrides, didn't particularly care about them one way or the other, but she cared about Jake. *A lot.* His past had clearly left a mark on him, but if his dad was clean and sober now, maybe Jake's visiting home would be healing. Or at least present an opportunity for closure.

Jake narrowed his eyes at her. "Did Grace put you up

to this? She's been after me in both direct and sneaky ways to spend time with them."

"No!" Brooke was insulted by the suggestion. "She didn't 'put me up' to anything. I just thought that it might be good for you to—"

Through gritted teeth, he made a sound of frustration. "I would think that you, of all people, would understand my position. Doesn't there come a time when you stop the insanity of trying to alter who people are and just take a step back? Live and let live?"

Brooke bit her bottom lip. To some extent, hadn't she tried to distance herself—emotionally as well as physically—from her family when she left for college and when she accepted Giff's proposal? Was she trying to replace her flawed family with the one she and Giff would build together? *The glossy, socially polished fantasy version.* The thought wasn't as soothing as it had been an hour earlier; instead, it made her feel vaguely ashamed.

She was quiet as Jake drove. They backtracked a few miles, going farther away from downtown Chattanooga and its most popular sites. They got lucky at a hotel off the interstate that was undergoing renovations.

"Several floors are under construction," the manager told them, "so we couldn't offer a big block of rooms to the people coming for the choir competition. And I have to warn you, it can get a little noisy with the power tools and whatnot during the day."

Brooke weighed the possibility of hammering and drills against the option of staying with Bob and Erma, and exchanged glances with Jake.

"We'll take it," he said as she nodded in vehement agreement. "Them, I should have said. You do have *two* rooms available?"

"Yes, sir. I can give you adjoining rooms on the second floor."

"Sounds perfect." Jake glanced behind the man at a stand of brochures about the local attractions. "And can we have a couple of those, too?"

Brooke pressed a hand to her chest, widening her eyes. "Surely you aren't going to stoop to looking at information about prices and operating hours and directions? That sounds dangerously like planning ahead."

He grinned at her. "Maybe just this once."

Chapter Twelve

Jake couldn't get comfortable. He was fidgety in the too-hot hotel room and wondered if Brooke noticed that this was the third time he'd lowered the air-conditioning. As he walked away from the thermostat and back to the upholstered chair, his conscience picked a fight with him. *It's only seventy-two degrees in here, and you've withstood blazing infernos and time in the desert. Your problem is not the temperature.*

Then a small devil appeared on Jake's shoulder and looked pointedly at the king-size bed that dominated most of the room.

I'm ignoring you, Jake informed both his scruples and his baser instincts. He was certainly *not* going to make a move on his best friend's girl. And since it was a nonissue, he had nothing to feel guilty about, either. *So, begone.*

Brooke, thank heavens, was occupied reading a brochure at the desk on the other side of the small room and didn't seem to realize that her traveling companion had lost his flipping mind.

She took her planning very seriously. After she'd

knocked on the door connecting their rooms, she'd suggested that since they only had one full day here—tomorrow—they rate the local sites in terms of priority.

"That way," she'd lectured, adorably earnest, "even if we run out of time before we leave on Saturday, you know you got to do the stuff you most wanted."

Not likely. Every time he glanced at her, he wrestled with the realization that what he wanted most might well be right in this room.

"Damn it!" Hadn't he just sworn that this wasn't a problem? That he could recognize how attractive Brooke was without being attracted *to* her? That he could enjoy her company platonically without becoming addicted to it and wanting more?

For the first time ever, Jake empathized with his father's alcoholism, with the self-destructive desire to have something you knew rationally you should leave the hell alone.

"Jake?" Brooke had glanced up, startled by his sudden oath.

"Sorry. Stubbed my toe." It was the best lie he could improvise, but still pretty absurd considering he was standing squarely between the dresser and the foot of the bed with absolutely nothing in his way. *Yes, the big studly fireman stubbed his toe on carpet fiber. That's plausible.* "Hey, are you hungry? We could run out and get an early dinner."

"I guess."

"You could bring all those brochures with us," he

cajoled, "and tell me about what you've learned so far."
Food and facts. And more importantly, miles between
them and this mocking king-size bed.

THEY FOUND A MODEST-LOOKING building with a hand-
painted sign that read simply Hamburger Shack. The
paper menus bore out that description. Entrées included
a three-cheese burger, buffalo burger, barbecue burger,
veggie burger and "chopped steak" salad. But what the
diner lacked in upscale decor or variety, it made up for
in taste.

"Wow," Jake said, surreptitiously double-checking
to make sure he didn't have mustard on the side of his
mouth. "This may even be better than the burgers at
Buck's."

Brooke blinked. "That's where my sister works. For
now, anyway. I'm surprised the two of you hadn't met
before the party. She *definitely* would have remembered
you. And she's not exactly forgettable herself."

"Umm."

"What?"

"Nothing, it will sound insulting and that's not what
I…"

She set her hamburger down. "Go ahead. I can take
it." She sounded oddly forlorn, rather than angry on her
sister's behalf.

After a moment, he laughed. "I'm not sure you understand. It's just, I'm sure your sister…?"

"Meg," she reminded him.

"Sorry. I knew that. I'm used to ranks and call signs.
I'm not as good with actual birth names. Anyway, I

know I met her at Grace's, and I recall that she was wearing something…bright. But that's about it." Nothing like his first meeting with Brooke, which he'd thought about in vivid detail afterward. He could still remember the stiff bearing of her shoulders that was so far removed from her casual, laughing demeanor as she'd teased him today or her fluid grace whenever she was on a dance floor.

He'd been trained to study situations and assess them for possible dangers; Meg, from what he could recall, was pretty, a bit flirty but essentially harmless, having no tactical impact on his life. Brooke, however, had been a threat to his peace of mind from the moment he saw her.

Sidestepping that explosive topic, Jake redirected the conversation to less personal matters. "Tell me about what you found in the brochures and we can start prioritizing."

"Well, the Incline Railway—which is the steepest passenger incline in the world—is open until about nine during the summer, so we might have time to do that after dinner. If you're interested," she added sheepishly.

"I'm interested."

"Tomorrow we could hit the aquarium or Lookout Mountain or try to squeeze in both. And I was reading about Ruby Falls—the cave with the underground waterfalls? The normal tour features music and theatrical lighting and geographical information, like the difference between a stalactite and a stalagmite. But they also offer another, more limited, lantern tour on certain nights. It's quieter and darker, except for the lanterns, and includes folktales and legends. The literature described it as a night of natural beauty and an aura of mystery, beginning with a 260-foot descent into the mountain."

"Sounds intriguing." The tour sounded fine, Jake supposed, but he was having a much stronger reaction to the idea of being in such close quarters with Brooke, surrounded by potentially romantic lighting. *Get a grip. It's a cave, not a candlelit four-star restaurant.* There was little chance she'd be overcome by the seductive atmosphere and throw herself at him.

Which left him simultaneously relieved and disappointed.

"I can call in the morning," she volunteered, "and see if we're too late to get tickets for tomorrow night."

He grinned at her efficient tone and all the facts she'd apparently memorized in such a short time. "You're very good at this. Ever think about becoming a travel agent instead of a journalist?"

She paused, as if debating her next words. "There was a time I considered both. Sort of. I wanted to be a travel writer, visit faraway places and bring them to life for other people who would never be lucky enough to see them. You know who Kira Salak is?"

He shrugged apologetically. "It's possible I've heard of her, but…bad with names, remember?"

"She's been all over the world, won writing awards. I wanted to be like her." Brooke laughed, but there was no humor in the sound. "Which sounds ridiculous when

I say it aloud. *She's* kayaked alone to Timbuktu, and you had to coerce me to get on a plane today just because it's smaller than what I'm used to. It's obvious I made the right career move, covering something safe like weddings and charity events rather than trying to chronicle a firsthand trip to the south pole or the Amazon."

The hollowness in her tone was unsettling. She was too young, with far too much still ahead of her, to sound so resigned over the way her life had turned out. Most beautiful women on the verge of marrying the man of their dreams would be ebullient.

"Who's to say you can't still follow long-ago dreams?" Jake demanded. "Maybe you won't go to the south pole. But that doesn't mean Giff won't take you to the south of France for your anniversary or some great Italian villa. Isn't there some kind of freelance market for travel pieces?"

"I—"

"Just look at this weekend," he interrupted. Granted, Tennessee might not have the same exotic cachet as, say, the African Serengeti or the Australian Outback, but everyone had to start somewhere. "You're taking a trip and writing about it!"

"Technically, I'm writing about *your* trip." Her lips quirked in a smile. "But I appreciate the thought. I didn't mean to sound defeatist when I was talking about the travel writing. That was just a crazy idea I had when I was younger. I have other goals now and I'm on the logical path to reaching them. I am very happy with my life."

Really? Because Jake had once caught an arsonist,

still holding the gas can, and even *his* protestations of innocence were more believable than Brooke's declaration.

AFTER SPENDING SEVERAL HOURS in the June heat, exploring Lookout Mountain on Friday, Brooke was blissfully appreciative of the aquarium's cool interior.

Despite the escalating temperatures, however, she'd had an amazing morning. She'd been alternately awed by the natural wonders—such as the Balanced Rock, billed as weighing a thousand tons, perched on two tiny rock points—and charmed by the more fanciful elements of their tour, such as the local legends about gnomes. Knowing how amused her mother would be by the stories, Brooke had even purchased a decorative gnome for her parents' yard, kind of a gag gift and the type of whimsical gesture Didi loved.

Brooke had been less charmed by Lovers' Leap. Oh, the view had been spectacular enough, but she'd cringed at the accompanying "romantic" legend of a Cherokee woman who'd been thrown off the edge because she dared love a man forbidden to her. According to folklore, the man had then jumped to his own demise, presumably so that they could be together in the hereafter.

One woman in oversize sunglasses and a UNC Tar Heels shirt had sniffed loudly at the story's conclusion. Brooke hadn't been able to stop herself from rolling her eyes.

"I take it," Jake had commented in a whisper, "that you're not impressed with the legend of the star-crossed maiden and brave?"

"Stories like that always make me feel like the grinch who stole Valentine's Day," Brooke had grumbled. "I remember having to read *Romeo and Juliet* in high school and all my girlfriends thought it was *so* moving. I was the killjoy who didn't get it. Okay, yes, Shakespeare had some great lines in that play and I've loved some of his other works, but…what was the takeaway, really? That if you truly love someone, you'd die without them? Melodramatic tripe."

"So you've never felt that way about anyone," Jake had concluded. "That you'd die without them?"

She'd had a fleeting impression of herself, at twenty, mooning over Sean the sexy poet. She'd definitely fallen under the delusion that she just *had* to be with him— idiotic, since he'd turned out to be a self-centered jerk who'd habitually asked her for loans and had caused her more disturbance than joy. She hadn't died without him, she'd thrived, reminded anew of how to make intelligent choices in her life. Ultimately, perhaps she should be grateful to him for helping make decisions that led her to Giff.

"Let's say I was thrown into an abyss," Brooke had hypothesized. "I am confident that Giff, much as he loves me, is far too rational to leap to his own doom. Why would I even want him to do that for me? It's inane. And I know that, should anything ever happen to him, he would want me to remember him well and move on with my life. Tossing yourself off a cliff or stabbing yourself with your lover's dagger is really just the cowardly way out."

Jake had stared at her for a long moment before agreeing, "Your outlook does sound more sensible."

"Thank you," she'd said uncertainly.

One could take his words as praise, yet something in his eyes kept them from being an outright compliment. She'd been curious to know what else he'd been thinking but had stopped herself from asking. Now, two hours later, they stood and watched frolicking river otters. The playful spectacle erased any lingering thoughts of her philosophy about lovers who threw themselves from precipices.

"I've always loved otters," she said.

"Really? They seem pretty...frivolous." Jake flashed her a teasing smile—she knew he was about to give her grief, but found herself grinning back rather than growing defensive. "I would have expected you to champion more serious, organized creatures."

She raised an eyebrow. "Such as?" Nothing that she knew of in the animal kingdom carried appointment books or smartphones. "You're going to say something like an ant or worker bee, aren't you?"

"I was thinking more like a lioness. They're smart, organized. They feed the pride, raise the young and take down animals bigger than themselves."

She'd assumed he was setting her up for good-natured mocking, and instead he'd compared her to a fierce, majestic animal? Not for the first time today, she felt as if she were tripping over her own expectations. *That's a man like Jake for you.*

He'd always keep a woman on her toes, never quite sure what to expect. It might be fun for an evening out or a road trip, but long term? It would be an unnerving, exhausting way to live, always trying to figure out the person you were with and never quite sure you had it right.

Then again, life with a man like Jake would have other perks.

Cheeks warming, she glanced away from him and toward the pond, making herself smile at the otters even though she wasn't really seeing them anymore.

"We should move on to the next exhibit so we don't cause a traffic jam," she muttered.

He gestured toward the door. "Lead on, Macduff. Although, technically, the original quote was 'lay on.'"

Brooke whipped her head around and stared.

"What?" He returned her gaze smugly. "You thought you were the only one to study Shakespeare in school? Most of A&M's degree plans are ranked in the national top ten. Besides…"

"Yes?"

"That commonly misquoted line from *Macbeth* was one of the tie-breaker questions last week at a trivia bar where some of us from the station hang out." Jake winked at her. "We got it wrong, but I always learn from my mistakes."

"Trivia bar?"

He nodded. "I don't subject myself to Karaoke on Saturdays, but I enjoy the trivia they do on weeknights. Plus they serve excellent buffalo wings."

"You had me going for a minute. I pictured you reading the Bard between calls at the firehouse."

"Truthfully, if I'm reading during my downtime, I

prefer a Jeff Shaara novel." They made their way into the multistoried central room where fiber-optic lights rippled like waves—the effect both soothing and dramatic. Ramps wound downward past huge tanks of fish, turtles and colorful coral. "What about you? You read a lot?"

"Mostly nonfiction," she said as they stopped to study some striped fish. Did her admission make her sound dull and unimaginative? Originally her problem had been just the opposite. "I used to make up lots of stories in my head, and whenever I read novels, my attention would wander. I'd take the characters and run with them, imagining what they looked like, which didn't always match the descriptions in the book, and what they'd say to me if they knew me. Ten minutes would pass and I'd realize that I hadn't even finished the page because I'd been dreaming up some adventure for me and whatever character instead of following the actual plot."

"How did you end up writing for a newspaper instead of spinning your own adventure tales?" Jake asked.

"I had to write book reports in elementary and middle school and chose nonfiction whenever possible because it helped me focus instead of getting carried away." *But only marginally.*

She omitted mention of the transcontinental flight she'd imagined herself taking with Amelia Earhart in the *Yellow Peril.* Any longing she'd had for such a trip had been cured by Boom's landing yesterday.

"I got interested in biographies and reading historical accounts by journalists of the day," she said, watching as graceful stingrays "flew" through the water. "I joined the seventh grade school paper and just followed that path."

"You were goal-oriented even in the seventh grade? I'm not sure whether that's admirable or a little eerie."

"It's not like I didn't experiment with other ideas along the way," she admitted. "I wrote a novel once. A very, very bad one."

Jake's eyebrows rose. "Really? When was this?"

"About ten years ago. College." She could feel her face heating as she recalled some of the more torrid passages. At the time, she'd considered the sensuality of her prose daring and cutting-edge, on par with great works that had spent time on the banned-books list. In retrospect, her writing had been overwrought and painfully girlish. "I was…going through a phase."

"What was the book about?"

"I aimed for epic historical literature and fell short. Oh, look, there's the moray eel!" She pointed. "I see where it's hiding now."

Next to her, Jake chuckled. It was a soft sound, nearly drowned out by the conversations buzzing around them, but he was standing so close she could almost feel the vibration of his body as he laughed.

"You're not going to tell me any more about the book, are you?"

"Not in this lifetime. Or any future lives, for that matter. Really, the scathing rejection letter I got was a blessing. I can't imagine how humiliated I'd be if that 'book' was available for people to actually read. The rejection did me the double favor of also being so contemptuous that I resumed my original course, getting serious about a career in journalism."

They were headed for the Ocean Journey exhibit when a toddler ran in the wrong direction, up the ramp and barreled past Brooke. He was followed by a mother frantically trying to catch him who bumped into just as many passersby as her son. Jake reached out to steady Brooke, his hand at her waist, making sure she didn't fall. Simply a precautionary measure, since neither the woman nor the little boy had jostled her that hard.

"You okay?" Jake asked, although she was clearly fine. She hadn't even lost her balance.

But the touch of his hand, warm through the light-weight fabric of her shorts, was enough to make her dizzy. It called to mind his arms around her as they'd danced at the engagement party. The way he'd felt when their bodies brushed, the way he'd looked at her.

"I—I'm good," she said, her breathless delivery at odds with her words.

He hadn't moved his hand yet, hadn't stepped back— not that he had room to move very far. Ironically the high volume of people on the ramp made her feel more alone with him, as the crush of pedestrians squeezed them against the rail in a seemingly isolated bubble.

"We shouldn't just be standing here," she heard herself say. The declaration sounded impressively casual. It didn't hint that, in her mind, things left unsaid rioted. *We shouldn't touch. We shouldn't have so much fun together. We shouldn't...*

"Right this way." Jake finally lifted his hand from her hip but then dropped both palms on her shoulders, gently steering her forward even while keeping her close in front of him. Because of the crowd, she reminded herself. And the limited space.

What if it's more than that? Was she impossibly conceited to think that this gorgeous man who'd been Giff's best friend for more than twenty years might be looking for an excuse to touch her?

Once they'd reached the bottom, he resumed an impersonal distance. She sighed, annoyed with herself for blowing an innocuous moment out of proportion. Just because she'd been explaining her previously overactive imagination was no reason to start indulging it again.

"Hmm." From behind her, Jake leaned forward so that he could better read the informational placards in front of the tank.

Brooke breathed in the scent of him, marveling that the simple act of inhaling could make her feel so guilty. She knew the brand name of the cologne that Giff favored, and she was pretty sure she liked it. But she was hard-pressed to remember how it smelled. Flutters of panic trembled through her midsection. Why was she able to remember her one close dance with Jake with more clarity than the many kisses she'd exchanged with her fiancé?

"Says here that they've acquired several new species of sharks."

A sand tiger shark, peering at them with its dead eyes, flicked its tail and came toward the glass right where Brooke stood.

"Creepy," she declared, mesmerized despite herself. "But kind of awesome at the same time."

The smile in his voice was evident when Jake said, "We'll make an adventurer of you yet. Sharks and the swing-along bridge in one day?" He referred to the one-hundred-and-eighty-foot bridge they'd used to cross over a gorge this morning.

Nudging her with his shoulder, he asked, "Does this mean you're becoming more open to taking chances?"

She glanced back but immediately wished she hadn't, afraid of what he might read in her eyes. "Probably not." After two relatively joyful days, she was forced to admit that occasional spontaneity could be diverting. But that didn't justify doing something as stupid as taking chances with her heart. *Or Giff's.*

"Jake. I—" She hadn't even realized she was backing away from him until she bumped into the railing between visitors and glass. She swallowed, unsure how to proceed.

"I have a confession to make," Jake said in a low voice.

"Y-you do?"

"Yeah. I hope it won't make you think less of me, but… Watching these fish and crustaceans all day? I'm craving seafood for lunch."

Her legs sagged in relief. *That* was his admission?

"I know, I know," he was saying, "I should be appreciating the beauty of nature and feeling a renewed determination toward protecting the environment. And I do feel all of that. But man I could go for some crab legs and shrimp. Have I horrified you?"

"Yes, I'm scandalized and will probably need therapy

to recover from the trauma," she drawled, amazed that she could joke when the truth was, she wanted to duck into a nearby darkened corner and have a good cry. Even though he'd given her no overt reason to think it, she'd somehow drawn the conclusion that he'd wanted to kiss her and might be working his way up to divulging that.

The hell of it was, she had no idea what she would have done if he had.

Chapter Thirteen

"Jake?" Giff's voice through the phone lines held no trace of the hostility from their post-party argument, but it was full of surprise. "It's so weird that you're calling. I just got off the phone with Brooke."

"Oh?" Jake sat heavily on the foot of the bed, glancing at the door that separated him and Brooke. "What did she have to say about the trip?"

"She *said* she's having a good time," Giff began dubiously, "but something in her voice... She wasn't herself. Is she upset for some reason? You aren't giving her a hard time, are you?"

"I am, but only in jest. And trust me, she gives back as good as she gets." He grinned, recalling some of her feistier quips this morning. "I respect that in a woman."

"Just be careful, will you? She takes things more seriously than you do. I don't want you unintentionally hurting her feelings."

Jake envisioned the look she'd given him in front of the shark tank today, the wounded wariness in her blue eyes. Had he hurt her already?

Disgust with himself made his voice rough. "I realize chivalry is your thing and I'm sure the ladies appreciate that, but has it ever occurred to you that it's not healthy for her—for anyone—to take life so seriously all of the time? Maybe she just needs…"

"She's perfect the way she is," Giff said loyally.

Incongruously Jake strongly disagreed and yet somehow thought his friend was completely right. Brooke had her flaws, but he was coming to enjoy them. *If I could change any one thing about her, I'm not sure I would.*

"I should be getting back to work," Giff said.

"It's five o'clock on a Friday, man. Why not kick off your weekend?" Jake had been thinking that Brooke didn't need to be so serious and cautious all of the time, but it would do Giff a world of good to have someone shake his life up a little, too.

"But it's only four in Denver, and I have a client there that I've been meaning to call all day. I told you how much business has picked up lately." Giff had explained that since some companies were trying to save money by reducing full-time positions in-house, it had actually created a few new short-term opportunities for independent contractors. "Oh, but before I let you go, I talked to Mom today. She asked you to bring her back some postcards. And you know her birthday's coming up this week, right?"

"Absolutely. We taking her to Santa Lucia's?" Whenever Jake was stateside and Giff was in town, they always took Grace to her favorite Italian restaurant for her birthday. "The three of us going there is tradition."

"Four of us now," Giff said. "Brooke will be joining us."

Of course she would. From here on out, she would be at dinners and holiday gatherings. Within Jake's life but out of his reach.

He swallowed hard. "Speaking of dinner. Brooke and I should be going, too. Did she tell you about our plans for tonight?"

"Something about a lantern-lit cave," Giff said distractedly. The sound of computer keys being struck accompanied his words. He was probably answering an e-mail while he talked.

Pay attention, Jake wanted to shout at him. *Turn off your computer and ask yourself why you're working on a Friday night while another man is about to take your beautiful fiancée out for the evening.* But he couldn't say that because Giff would point out that he trusted Jake completely.

Giff had always been too damn decent for his own good.

"MIND IF, INSTEAD OF USING the AC, we roll down the windows?" Brooke asked. As much as she legitimately wanted to feel the fresh air against her face, the request was also an excuse to simply say *something*. Neither of them had spoken two words since leaving Ruby Falls. The tour had been well-staged, but the deliberately ethereal atmosphere had only added to her jumpy, restless mood.

"Sounds good," Jake said, turning off the air-conditioning.

As he lowered the power windows, the sound of

the wind escalated until it filled the interior of the car. Brooke should have felt grateful. The noise gave them an excuse not to talk. Tomorrow, they left for Texas. If she could just get home without saying something stupid, something she wouldn't be able to take back...

But today had proven that feelings didn't simply go away if she refused to voice them. They kept circling, waiting to strike.

Dinner had started out all right. Despite some initial tension, she'd relaxed after a glass of wine and Jake had made her laugh. She'd enjoyed the great meal and even better company up until dessert, when she'd had the traitorous thought that the night was one of the best dates she'd had in years. Immediately she'd tried to backpedal and assure herself that it hadn't been a *date*. But, while neither she nor Jake had said anything inappropriate, she couldn't deny a flirtatious undertone between them.

A spark.

Jake was a fireman. She was sure he could attest to the fact that sparks seemed bright and exciting, until they made contact and burned your life down around you.

As if he could feel her growing trepidation, Jake cut his eyes toward her. "Are you okay? I called Giff earlier, and he asked if maybe you were upset about something."

"I called Giff, too." *Guilty minds think alike?* Or was the disturbing chemistry she felt with Jake one-sided, leaving him with a clear conscience?

"He mentioned. I'm sure he was glad to hear from you. Probably misses you."

"I've only been gone since yesterday," she scoffed. Feeling defensive that *she* hadn't missed Giff more, she added, "I don't think I could marry a man so needy that he fell apart without me after forty-eight hours."

"You can miss someone without 'falling apart,'" Jake objected. "You can hear a joke you want to share with them, want to make them laugh. You can think about what they were wearing the last time you saw them and look forward to your next meeting. You can replay pieces of conversation in your head and appreciate someone who makes you see the world a little bit differently."

He'd done more than slightly alter her view of the world; he'd blown her world off its axis with nuclear force.

"Jake," she said warningly. Her heart was racing. At the aquarium, she'd been able to convince herself that whatever moment she'd dreamt up between them had been a product of her imagination. But she wasn't imagining the intensity of his voice.

"I think about you when you're not there," he admitted hoarsely.

He slowed down to take the turn into the hotel parking lot, and for a moment Brooke's instinct to flee was so strong that she entertained the notion of jumping from the moving vehicle. Not just because of what she was afraid he might say next, but because it was becoming impossible to pretend that *she* didn't think about him constantly.

"The week after we went to that concert?" he pressed. "One of the guys at the station was playing a CD I'd never heard before, and I found myself wondering what you'd think of the band. And that day you came to see me after that little girl was hit? I thought about you all night. Every time I was frustrated that I couldn't do more to help her, worried that she might take a turn for the worse... I don't know. Remembering your visit and knowing you were there for me—"

"Stop," she pleaded.

"Are you saying we can't be friends?"

"Do you talk to all your 'friends' like this?" she snapped, her eyes stinging. She barely heard the catch in her own voice.

He parked the car, and Brooke tried to follow through on her impulse to run from what she was feeling. But her vision was blurred and her hands shook as she wrestled with the seat belt.

"Here." Reaching over, Jake pressed the button that freed her. But then he lifted his finger to her cheek, brushing away a tear with paralyzing tenderness. "Please don't cry."

"I wasn't looking for... I would never..." She hiccupped, the sound reminding her distantly of Didi and the way her mother always got the hiccups during her crying jags.

No, no, no! Brooke didn't want drama and crying and that ridiculous have-to-have-you-or-I'll-die passion. She wanted...

Involuntarily she turned to look at Jake, his profile as familiar and dear to her as if she'd known him her whole life rather than just a month. Right now, his handsome features were strained with worry and anger. She found herself wanting to take him in her arms and console him even though *she* was the one crying.

He must have been having the same reaction because he scooted closer to her, the proximity made awkward because of the armrest and parking brake. Then he put his arm around her, pressing her head to his shoulder.

"I know," he murmured.

And she believed he truly did understand what she was experiencing even though she'd yet to express an articulate thought.

She closed her eyes and took a deep breath, accepting his comfort for just a second, allowing herself this luxury before reason returned. Once it did, she had to tell him that this was a mistake, that they should make an effort not to be in the same room with each other for at least a little while. Maybe the next forty or fifty years.

When she opened her eyes again, it was to find Jake with his head tilted back against the seat, meeting her gaze with disconcerting intimacy. He was far too close. And yet it took everything in her not to wiggle closer to him. It would only be a matter of breaths before her lips met his.

Obviously she had no poker face because no sooner had she had the thought than his gaze dropped to her mouth. Heat flooded her body.

And remorse flooded her mind.

Brooke straightened abruptly. "We would both hate ourselves. And I'd have to bear the responsibility of not just betraying a man I care deeply about but of coming between the two of you. You love Giff like a brother," she reminded him.

"Do you?" Jake challenged. "Love him, I mean?"

For a nanosecond, she was so filled with outrage that she wanted to strike out at him. But she'd worked her entire adult life to sublimate emotion to sensibility. As a result, she sounded credibly calm when she said, "I have to go."

"That's not an answer." His voice was more broken than accusatory.

She didn't look back as she opened the car door. "It's the only one I can give you."

BY NOON SATURDAY, JAKE was sick of his own company and spoiling for a fight. The only interaction he'd had with Brooke all day was the voice mail she'd left on his hotel phone. He couldn't believe that it was coincidence she'd happened to call during the ten minutes he was in the shower. Had she been lying awake in the room next door, listening for the sound of the pipes?

What the message said, technically, was, "It's Brooke. I know we had an itinerary for this morning, but I didn't get much rest last night. I think I'm just going to sleep in. You go on without me and I'll meet you in the lobby at checkout time."

What the message *meant* was, "You are an unscrupulous bastard in complete violation of the bro-code, and I am more comfortable avoiding my feelings than confronting you." Both sentiments were unfortunately accurate.

Fine. He was better off without her disturbing his

calm anyway. After all, he made most of these trips by himself and had always found them rejuvenating. It wouldn't bother him in the least to have a few hours to himself.

Or, it shouldn't have. But it wasn't the same, aimlessly sightseeing without Brooke keeping him on schedule and snapping dozens of pictures with her digital camera. Yesterday, an elderly woman had offered to take a picture for Brooke. "Of you and your boyfriend, dear. Darn shame such a good-looking couple isn't in the shot together." Brooke had blushed furiously, explaining that they weren't romantically involved, that she was "only here on business."

Truthfully, he'd found himself stung by her instantaneous denial of any personal bond.

Last night he'd proven there was something between them. What had it really accomplished, though? He'd tried to push her into admitting that her feelings for Giff didn't run that deep—not deep enough to spend an entire lifetime together—but all he'd succeeded in doing was pushing her away. Plus he'd stabbed his friend in the back in the process.

I am a real piece of work. He heard long-ago criticisms from his dad, drunken predictions that Jake was a pain in the ass who wouldn't amount to anything. Ironically those memories didn't burn as much as the recollection of Giff's father, Mr. Baker, smiling at Jake in pride. *He believed in me.* And how had Jake repaid that faith—by making a play for Giff's soon-to-be wife?

They shouldn't be getting married at all, an inner voice stubbornly insisted. *They're making a mistake.*

And Jake should know. He was fast becoming an expert on mistakes.

THOUGH SHE'D BOUNCED AROUND between several different cities in the state, Brooke had lived in Texas since the eighth grade. Seeing the aerial view as Boom lowered their altitude reminded her how flat the state was—except for the aptly named Hill Country. Long rural stretches, punctuated below by patchwork pastureland, suddenly gave way to concrete labyrinths like Dallas or Houston. It reminded her of some grandiose monstrosity of architecture that had been cobbled together in contrasting styles but was uniquely beautiful despite itself. Texas had definitely become home.

And it was where she planned to build her future home, raising her own children. Normally thoughts like that worked as meditation. She wished she could close her eyes, hold her breath for twenty beats and let the promise of a cherished future soothe her abraded nerves. But the faces of her storybook children, the ones she'd all but named in her imagination, were now indistinct, the picture fuzzy as if she had bad cable reception.

She fought the urge to glare at Jake. Not so much because the gesture would be petty—it wasn't as if she herself was blameless in their unfortunate attraction— but because he would no doubt notice. For the most part, they'd successfully ignored each other since leaving the hotel, and she didn't want to do anything to alter that.

She was so tied up in knots that this time she barely

noticed when the plane touched down on the runway. *Thank God.* Their weekend together was over.

Except, of course, for the extremely awkward car ride still ahead. What were the odds that Houston traffic would be sparse, with no detours, motor vehicle accidents or construction delays?

Determined not to rock the boat, she didn't protest when Jake grabbed her rolling suitcase, even though she could have just as easily got it herself. Nor did she say anything when he opened the passenger door for her, although she did hold herself involuntarily rigid as she passed by him.

They'd only made it to the edge of the parking lot before he asked with deceptive nonchalance, "So, when will the story run?"

"Depends on a few factors, but probably Friday." The idea of writing it, of sorting through the many pictures she'd taken of him and capturing details of their trip for posterity, made her cringe inwardly.

She'd much rather forget the past couple of days had ever happened. She would prefer to go back to the mature, sensible person she'd been when she boarded Boom's Skyhawk, instead of rediscovering a foolish girl who'd felt too passionately and dreamed too ambitiously.

This isn't college. Brooke was a grown woman capable of making intelligent decisions.

"And then I guess it's back to the weddings beat?" he asked, his smile approximately the same temperature as an ice cube.

"That's right. Beginning with *my* wedding."

"To Giff." Jake's fingers clenched around the steering wheel. "You really think this marriage is fair to him?"

"How dare you! I will do everything I can to be an excellent wife."

"Would you characterize yourself as an excellent fiancée?" Jake challenged. "Even though you have feelings for someone else?"

Panic flared within her. Was he threatening to tell Giff what had happened? *Nothing happened! You did the right thing and walked away, and now you're paying for his damaged ego.* "You're making an awful big assumption about my 'feelings.' Trust me, any fleeting confusion I experienced is becoming less of an issue by the moment. I'm not one of those bad-boy magnets who gets hot and bothered over guys who act like jerks." Her experiences in her twenties had cured her of that.

"You think I'm a jerk just because I have the cojones to tell you the truth?" Jake snapped. "You don't want a husband, you want a human security blanket."

Her hand flew to her abdomen as if she were trying to block a blow. "*Excuse* me?" She'd known Jake was ticked off; she hadn't realized he had such a repugnant opinion of her.

"Last night, you couldn't even tell me you loved Giff." He never took his eyes off the road as he changed lanes, but she felt as if he was staring at her and could see into all the exposed corners where she was vulnerable.

"That's because I don't owe you any explanations!"

"You talk about your parents and sister like you're the de facto sane limb on the family tree, but you're not just sensible, you're scared. Afraid you'll end up like them, maybe even afraid of repeating past mistakes of your own."

"Learning from a person's mistakes doesn't make them a coward, it means they have *common sense!*"

"What about giving up on a dream at the first hint of a setback? Honestly, Brooke, did you ever consciously think to yourself that you wanted a career writing about the taffeta and chiffon choices of Sugar Land brides, or was it just the least threatening option?"

"Well, we can't all charge headfirst into blazing buildings," she retorted, "but it's a living."

"Really? That's really your idea of a life, following the paths of least resistance and never caring enough about anything to risk—"

"Oh, *I'm* the coward?" she asked, goaded beyond all resistance. "Remind me, when was the last time you had your dad over for a cookout?"

The blood drained from his face. For a split second, he was so pale that she worried if she'd upset him too badly for him to drive safely. But then he regained his composure.

"Well, I guess I'm not the only one with cojones, after all," he said, his tone still mad but now respectful, too.

"Sorry." Just because Jake was getting too personal didn't mean she should have abandoned her self-control.

"Don't be. That's the kind of raw honesty found in real relationships. You and Giff don't argue, you each support anything the other says because he's too afraid of being alone and not having a family and you're too afraid to allow yourself to feel anything messy."

"If you're quite finished, Dr. Phil, you missed my street."

He flipped on his blinker and did a U-turn.

She was literally trembling with fury. Did Jake McBride honestly think he had all the answers? By his own admission, he wasn't dating anyone and had never been in a truly serious relationship. That "raw honesty" philosophy he spouted could become warped into a justification for saying hurtful things, for slamming doors and otherwise acting out like an uncivilized toddler rather than "repressing" emotions. Her parents' marriage had been plenty raw, and she had no intention of inflicting similar circumstances on her own children. Or herself.

"You're right," Jake said suddenly, his soft tone a sharp contrast to their previously raised voices.

I am? Brooke blinked. "About?"

"Me, my family. I'm scared to hope that he's better because I've been disappointed before, scared to hope that we can be more than we are. But being around you… You make me hope fiercely for things I didn't even know I wanted."

She squeezed her eyes shut. This was so much worse than when he'd been provoking an argument with her; this was impossible to combat. "We went through this last night."

"Not really. You left before we'd finished the conversation," he reminded her. He pulled up in front of her apartment building and turned off the ignition.

"I can get the suitcase," she chirped, bolting from the car. "No need for you to get out of…"

But she was fighting a losing battle and didn't bother to say anything else as Jake saw her to her door. He even towed it inside to the foyer. She wondered if a bright smile and a "have a nice life!" would prompt him to leave, but she doubted it.

So instead she crossed her arms across her chest. "He's your best friend. How can you do this to him?" she demanded.

"He deserves to find someone who loves him, really loves him. That's the one percent of me that's being noble. The other ninety-nine wants to kiss you so bad I can't even think."

Her heart pounded in her ears, and her palms went clammy. *I want him, too.* It was selfish of her and went against all her careful planning, yet she found herself leaning, swaying almost imperceptibly toward him.

Since he'd been watching her with the hungry intensity of a predator about to pounce, he caught her movement. It was all the permission he needed before folding his arms around her and lowering his mouth to hers. The shock of their lips meeting sizzled through her, but she didn't have time to process it. It wasn't a quick peck, it was an unending onslaught of sensation. Clinging to him, she kissed him back for all she was worth, swept up in desire—the way he felt against her, the way he tasted—that verged on bewildering. How had she forgotten that kissing could make her feel like this? *Had* kissing ever made her feel like this?

Need ran sharply through her, so keen it was almost

physically painful. It wasn't until her knees threatened to buckle that she was able to reassert her sense of self-preservation. *What in the* hell *am I doing?*

She twisted away from him, trying to ignore the swollen feel of her lips and the tingling in her breasts.

"Brooke, I—I didn't intend for that to be so aggressive."

"The problem's not with the *kind* of kiss! It's that I kissed you in the first place." She flashed her left hand between them, drawing both of their gazes to the engagement ring.

"You're planning to go through with it, then?"

How could she?

How could she not?

"I don't know." She strode past him and yanked open the door. "But whether I do or not, I don't ever want to be alone with you again. Goodbye, Jake."

Chapter Fourteen

Oh, God, oh, God, oh, God. Brooke stood against the closed door, wringing her hands like a bad actress in a melodrama. She wasn't this person. She was paralyzed by the nauseating indecision over what to do next—confess all to Giff immediately or spend the next seventy years hoping he never found out. *I can't face him.*

Which might make for an awkward ceremony.

If this is what cheating felt like, why did anyone ever do it? Her mind flickered briefly to Jake's devastating kisses. All right, she wasn't completely naive as to why people might stray. But how on earth did they live with themselves afterward?

Damn you, McBride. This was exactly the sort of upheaval she'd always wanted to steer clear of—and she couldn't stand the idea that her bad decision would bring upheaval to *Giff's* life.

Tears pricked her eyes. Suddenly Brooke had a thought she hadn't consciously entertained since she'd broken her arm roller-skating at age nine—she wanted her mother. The benefit of Didi's less-than-orthodox life was that not much shocked her and she had plenty of experience to draw from. Perhaps she could help Brooke sort through the fallout of what she'd done.

It was enough of a plan to motivate her to move from the foyer to the phone in her living room. She dropped onto the couch and dialed her parents' number. Would they be home on a Saturday night?

After three rings, the answering machine picked up, but the outgoing message wasn't the familiar "You've reached Didi and Everett." Instead, there was a giggle, followed by Didi's voice.

"Hola! You have *not* reached the Nichols…because we're out of town for a few days. Oh, but don't bother casing the joint because we have nothing worth stealing. Leave a message after the beep and we'll try to call you back next week! *Adios, amigos."*

Brooke disconnected the call, momentarily baffled. Judging by her mother's announcement—*who tells random callers that the house is sitting vacant, for crying out loud?*—Didi and Everett had gone to Mexico. She shouldn't be surprised. How many spur-of-the-moment adventures had peppered her childhood? But just last weekend, she'd been seriously worried that her parents' marriage might be in jeopardy.

When, in fact, it was her own love life that had plummeted in a flaming, downward spiral.

Her curiosity getting the better of her, she punched in the number for her mom's cell phone.

"Buenas noches! Brooke, is that you, dear?" Without waiting to confirm that she was talking to her daughter, Didi enthused, "You'll never believe where we are.

Cancún! Your father booked us into a great resort. We've eloped."

"Again?"

"Well, last time we eloped and got married. This time we eloped to our honeymoon."

"A long, overdue honeymoon," declared Everett from somewhere in the background. Then he added something else that was muffled, prompting a delighted chuckle from Didi and what might have been a kiss.

"Mom?" Given the night she'd had, Brooke didn't think she could handle listening to her parents make out over the phone.

"Right here! Anyway, as I was explaining, your father and I were talking about your wedding, all the details we skimped on."

Brooke nodded, then felt silly as she realized no one could actually see her. "I remember you being upset about that at the engagement party."

"Well, your father felt awful that he might not have shown me how important our marriage is to him, so he said that there was at least one neglected detail we could take care of now. And here we are in Cancún! Isn't he the most romantic man in the world?"

"I'm glad the two of you are having fun. But, Mom, telling everyone on your machine that you're away—"

"You worry too much. Didn't you hear the part where I told would-be thieves there was nothing good in the house anyway? The only thing our family ever had of substantial value was each other."

"Wow." Brooke wiped her eyes with the back of her hand. "That's really beautiful, Mom."

"I meant it! I have to go, but I'll call you when we get back. Give Giff our love, okay?"

It was then that Brooke realized she hadn't even broached the topic of why she was calling.

Judging by the dial tone buzzing in her ear, however, it was too late. And she was still drowning in the need to talk to someone. Kresley? Nah, it was getting a bit late in the evening to call the mommy-to-be. At least, that was what Brooke rationalized when she balked at the thought of admitting her wrongdoings to her stable, married, pregnant friend—the woman who had everything Brooke had thought she wanted.

She slid the engagement ring off of her finger, staring intently at the diamond as if she could see the future in it. For all that she'd derided some of her parents' choices, Didi had sounded so ecstatic on the phone, so full of pure, unadulterated joy. Brooke didn't have that with Giff. She had…contentment. She'd convinced herself that not only was it enough, it was preferable.

What if Giff thought differently? What if he, as Jake said, deserved someone who felt more for him and one day resented Brooke's emotional lack?

She dialed Meg's cell phone, mainly to keep herself from doing something rash and calling Giff before she'd worked out what to say to him. She knew her sister was waitressing tonight and simply left a message asking her to call if she had a break. Retaining at least a modicum of emotional self-discipline, Brooke avoided the phrase *end of the world* in her recording, even though it felt accurate.

She brushed her teeth and had just changed into a

baggy burnt-orange Texas Longhorns sweat suit when Meg called back.

"Hey, little sister. Can you hear me? I'm in the employee break room, which is really a glorified supply closet, but it's a lot quieter than out on the floor. Plus I get to sit down back here. My feet are killing me! I don't know what I'm going to do next, but my days as a waitress are numbered, mark my words. So…you rang? I assume you're trying to find out about Mom and Dad."

"Actually, I talked to her earlier tonight and that situation seems pretty self-explanatory. They've made up and decided to make sudden use of their passports. She sounded happy," Brooke admitted, pulling back her comforter and wondering if anyone would notice if she hid out in bed for a week.

Not that she was a coward, she told herself, annoyed at the memory of Jake's mocking tone. She was just suddenly more tired than she could ever remember feeling.

"Doesn't she?" Meg was agreeing. "You gotta admit, Mom and Dad's dysfunctional cycle seems to work for them. I know you and Giff are probably too civilized for this, but a lot of couples grow closer after fighting. They air their differences in a cleansing, blow-out argument, then get to make up. Some people even think of it as forepl—"

"Don't say it," Brooke begged. Meg would think she was being squeamish about the idea of their parents in a sexual relationship, but Brooke was struggling not to dwell on her own appalling behavior. One minute, she and Jake had been hollering at each other in his car; the next, they'd been making out in her doorway.

"You don't have to sound so repelled by the idea," Meg chided lightly. "To each her own. Like I said, I doubt you and Giff will ever fight. Y'all don't have that kind of—"

"Raw honesty?"

"I might have said raw chemistry, but close enough."

"Meg, if I tell you something…"

"Ooh, this sounds intriguing! You're not about to rock my world with some dark secret about you and Giff, are you?"

Brooke stared at the ceiling. "You're half-right. You remember his friend Jake McBride, the best man? He kissed m— *We* kissed," she amended, wanting to own up to her share of the blame for what had taken place.

"*What?* When?"

Brooke gave her sister the thumbnail rundown of the past two days. In retrospect, the kiss seemed almost inevitable. The events leading up to it were so clear that Brooke was angrier at herself for letting it all fall into motion. Why hadn't she kept better distance at the aquarium, said no to the mellowing wine at dinner and the flirty banter that followed? Why had she stayed in the car so long last night once the conversation lapsed into the inappropriate?

Perhaps most upsetting of all—why had she hesitated so blatantly when Jake had asked if she loved Giff?

"I don't," she heard herself say aloud. "I don't truly love Giff, not passionately."

"Well, I could have told you that! Wait," Meg said. "I *did* tell you that. I'm so glad you finally decided to listen. This means you'll call off the wedding, right?"

"Megan, could you try to sound a little less gleeful about all of this?"

"Sorry. But you *are* going to break the engagement?"

The idea of undoing all of their careful plans left a cold knot of fear in Brooke's chest. "What will we tell his mother? She'll hate me." That prospect hurt as much as the idea of Giff hating her. *Definite red flag.* A bride should not be more emotionally invested in the groom's family than the man himself.

Still, even now that she had no choice but to admit that the wedding was a mistake, it seemed too overwhelming to halt. "The invitations have been mailed! And you and I finally found a dress we agreed on."

Since it was supposed to have been a small wedding and the other bridesmaid would be in a maternity dress, Brooke had decided simply to help her sister pick out a department store formal. Needless to say, she and Meg had possessed different ideas about what would be a good look for the ceremony.

"I get where you're coming from," Meg sympathized. "You've put a lot of work into this. But I'm pretty sure that his mom, my dress and some postmarked envelopes are *not* a reason to pledge the rest of your life to someone."

"You're absolutely right."

"Who'd have thunk it?" Meg asked cheerfully. "Me, giving words of wisdom. And I guess this means you're no longer the predictable sister. Want to borrow back that leather top?"

"Borrow?" Somehow, in spite of the way she was feeling, Brooke managed to laugh. "You mean the one that belongs to me? Thanks, but no. I think I'm going to be in more of a curl-up-in-sweat-socks kind of mood for a while."

"For a guy like Jake, I personally would make a little more effort, but if you—"

"Effort?" Brooke sat bolt upright. "Megan, I'm not going to see him again." That might be the one positive thing that came from breaking off the engagement with Giff, freeing herself from Jake's challenging presence and disturbingly sexy kisses.

"But—"

"No! He's everything I don't want in a man."

Meg scoffed. "I don't think we're talking about the same guy."

"Thanks for listening, Meg, but I should let you get back to work so you don't get in trouble."

"Pfft. Most people are done with dinner now, we're just making rounds to refill drinks. Which I will go do, but don't think I can't recognize that you're blowing me off because you don't want to talk about Jake. Can I just say, for the record, that I think you're making a mistake?"

"You can. But you're wrong," Brooke said firmly.

"Don't be so quick to decide. After all, I was right about Giff being a mistake, wasn't I?"

Once they got off the phone, Brooke turned off her bedside lamp and lay in the dark, unable to sleep. Giff shouldn't have been a mistake. He should have been perfect for her. Where had she gone so disastrously wrong? She was blowing her chance to build exactly the life she'd always wanted with a great guy any woman would be lucky to have.

Not long before sunrise, she fell into fitful dreams. After a few hours of dozing and waking, each time to an increasing sense of dread, she decided to give up. She wasn't going to rest until she talked to Giff.

"Hello?"

The sound of his familiar voice made her stomach turn. *He doesn't deserve this.* "Hey. It's me. I…didn't wake you, did I?" There was a chance he'd been taking the opportunity to sleep in on a Sunday morning.

"Not at all. Been up doing some troubleshooting for a client. I was going to call you in another hour or so and ask if you wanted to have lunch today."

"I…" Would it be better to tell him in person or let him absorb the news now in the privacy of his own home, where he could rant and rave without an audience? Not that she could imagine the gentlemanly Giff ranting at her.

"How was your trip?" he asked. "Was the landing last night smoother than the other one you told me about?"

To her abject horror, a sob escaped her.

"Brooke? What is going on? I thought the other day that you sounded upset. Tell me what's wrong so we can fix it."

"You can't." At least, not without a time machine and maybe not then. Kissing Jake had been one of the stupider things she'd ever done, but even if she could erase that moment, it didn't mean that marrying Giff was the right thing to do. Up until now, it had simply been the *easier* thing. The safe choice. "You deserve more than this."

"I will *kill* him!"

For a heart-stopping instant, Brooke thought that Giff had somehow figured out what had happened last night.

"Brooke, if Jake made you feel like you're not good enough or that we haven't known each other long enough—"

"Nothing like that. I've just realized that I'm, well, shallow."

"No, you're not. Trust me, I've met some materialistic women at the club and you're not like them."

"Not that kind of shallow. It's just that I don't allow myself to feel things very deeply, very intensely." It was a half truth. Because when she'd been in Jake's arms, her reactions had been extremely intense. "You should find a wife who can love with her whole heart."

There was only the sound of Giff's ragged breathing. He didn't seem to know what to say. Brooke empathized. She, too, was having difficulty choosing her words. On the one hand, she wanted to clear the air completely and confess that she'd kissed Jake. But did her impulse to blurt the rest of the story stem from doing the right thing or simply assuaging her guilt at Giff's expense?

"Are you sure this is about *you* not being passionate

enough?" Giff finally asked. "I know I spend half of our evenings out networking and I don't dance with you as much as I should. And even though we haven't made l—"

"Please stop! You are perfect. For some other woman."

There was a noise like he was grinding his teeth. "This just doesn't make sense. I saw you earlier this week and you were fine. We were making plans for reception food. Then you call me from Tennessee, clearly upset, and now… Something happened."

"I am so, so sorry." The words sounded empty compared to the damage she'd done. But she couldn't stop herself from saying them. "Really very sorry."

"Sorry enough to tell me the truth, all of it? Whatever it is, Brooke, I can handle it."

Chapter Fifteen

"You son of a bitch!" Giff was barely out of his car before he'd shouted the accusation. Then he was zooming across Jake's driveway and front yard with a determined speed he hadn't shown since they played high school football.

Jake, having just come out of his house for work, froze, too shocked to brace himself for the flying tackle to come. "Ooomph." Both men hit the dirt, and it distantly occurred to Jake that, one, it was a good thing he had spare uniforms inside and, two, he was going to be late for his shift.

Now that his initial surprise was subsiding, Jake's training kicked in and he quickly got to his feet, evading his infuriated friend. "So obviously she—"

"Don't! You do *not* get to talk about her," Giff ordered, sounding as militant and intimidating as the scariest drill sergeant ever had. "I was going to *marry* her."

"I know! And I'm sorry." Jake bobbed to the right. "I should never have laid a hand on her. But marrying her would have been a mistake. I know you, and you do not love her like that."

Giff lunged. "That's not your decision to make, you arrogant—"

"Will you stop?" Jake blocked a punch he no doubt deserved. "I don't want to hurt you."

"It's a little late for that," Giff roared, a blow glancing off Jake's shoulder as he turned his body to deflect. "Do you know how much I *trusted* you?"

The full enormity of what he'd done was more bruising than anything Giff could mete out physically so Jake stopped dodging. Giff was so startled that he lost his balance, nearly toppling into the grass.

"Fight back." Giff glared. "You owe me that."

"No. But take your best shot. I have that coming."

Suddenly Giff laughed, the sound harsh and jagged enough to grate cheese. "And to think *I'm* the one who asked you to take her to the concert. I'm the one who suggested she write the article. I wanted you two to *like* each other. Guess that worked out pretty well, huh?"

Jake was too miserable to say anything in his defense. Betraying his brother was indefensible. "If it helps, she never wants to lay eyes on me again."

"Neither do I." Giff brushed bits of grass off of his slacks and squared his shoulders, looking less like a mad man and more like himself. Except for the set of his jaw and the uncharacteristic coldness in his eyes. "Don't come to Santa Lucia's on Mom's birthday. That's a *family* dinner."

"Wow." Kresley squinted into the dim apartment, which was cavelike compared to the June sunshine behind her. "You said in your voice mail that you were fine, but you look like refried hell."

"Thanks." Lacking the energy to stand there and make small talk, Brooke retreated back to the couch where she'd spent several worthwhile hours crying, castigating herself and watching quality daytime television. She knew Kresley would follow her; she'd be too curious to resist. "So you got my message about breaking off the engagement with Giff and taking a personal day."

"Yeah, and about that…a *message?* I'm one of your best friends. Plus I'm nosy. It's a requirement for a career in journalism. You had to know I'd be over."

"I thought it would be after work, not your lunch hour. Otherwise I might have made more of an effort to clean up for you." But probably not.

Kresley sat on a chair, her expression growing more serious. "Honey, what happened? I've never heard of you guys fighting—over *anything*—and you're both too stable to get cold feet."

"Kres, let me ask you something. Do you and Dane ever fight?"

Her friend frowned. "Well, sure, sometimes. I've never stormed out and told him I'm moving back in with my parents, and he doesn't call me ugly names, but we disagree as much as any normal couple. Did I tell you some of the names he suggested for the baby? Honestly, any woman in her right mind would have argued with those!"

"Right." Brooke leaned her head back against the sofa cushions. "So you think it's normal for couples to fight sometimes. And Giff and I never fought about anything. I don't think Giff and I were a normal couple."

"So…you broke up because you never fight?"

"That, and I kissed his best friend."

Kresley started to shoot to her feet, but was thwarted by her lower-than-usual center of gravity. Instead, letting herself fall back in the chair, she squeaked, "You *what?* You're talking about Jake McBride, right? The one who was originally Satan's spawn because he hated you and was dead set against the wedding, then took you dancing and was judged to be a decent guy after all, and then… I sent you to Tennessee with him! Is that where you kissed? Oh, dear Lord, I've wrecked your marriage."

"Kres! Take a breath. This is not your fault. And, actually, we kissed right over there." She pointed toward the front door. "When he brought me home Saturday night. Yesterday, I told Giff that I didn't think I loved him enough to marry him."

"Ouch."

"It's not his fault, obviously." Brooke tunneled a hand through her unbrushed hair. "I'm defective or something. I've known since I graduated college what I was looking for in a man, and Giff fit the description to a tee."

Kresley was silent, pondering. Finally she offered, "Well, it's been a few years. People grow. Maybe he would have been right for you once, but you've changed. Or maybe you were wrong about what you wanted. Or maybe you made a mistake. Does it have to be irreversible? You and Jake *just* kissed, right?"

"Yeah." But since she hadn't done much more than

that with Giff, she didn't think he'd be very comforted by that.

Meg had mocked Brooke's decision to wait until the wedding night to make love to Giff, and Brooke realized now her sister had a strong point. It was fine to decide to wait—that was a personal decision—but shouldn't she have at least been more tempted? Shouldn't she have found herself fantasizing about the honeymoon to come? He was a gorgeous man and a decent kisser. Not in Jake's league, but—

"Aah!" She pressed her hands to her ears as if she could drown out her own trampy thoughts. "I am a bad person."

"Not usually. You can get a little cranky once a month and when a big deadline is approaching, but... Sorry." Kresley relented when she noticed that her teasing hadn't cajoled a smile. "I'm trying to help. You just tell me what I can do."

"Help me return gifts and put postage on handwritten notes of apology? I don't know. I've never screwed up this big." Even when she'd been blinded by lust—which she'd confused with love—over Sean and let herself fall behind in classes, she'd had the excuse of youth. And she'd only hurt herself. This time she was a mature woman who'd hurt a good man. "I've never had to fix anything of this magnitude!"

No wonder Didi and Meg gave in to occasional hysteria. Even though it had often looked to Brooke like attention-seeking lack of control, she had newfound tolerance for them. And for their screwups. She was still baffled as to how she'd messed up her life so spectacularly despite having the best of intentions and a solid plan.

"I'm going to have to see Giff," she said. "I need to give him the ring back. He's way too chivalrous to ask for it, but I can't keep it! And at some point, I have to talk to his mother, though Lord knows what I'll say."

"I don't envy you either task." Kresley bit her lip. "If you don't mind my asking, what about Jake?"

Brooke sighed heavily. "Yeah, it won't be easy for him to face the Bakers, either. Giff sounded like he was seething when he got off the phone with me."

"I can imagine, but that's not what I meant. What about you and Jake? You planning to…talk to him again?"

"Oh. No." Brooke looked away, trying not to think about Jake. That way lay madness. "Not unless I have to e-mail him a follow-up question before we print the story. He's not looking for a girlfriend—said so himself. He has an erratic schedule and likes to travel alone. And, even if he was, can you *imagine* the complications? He and Giff have been best friends forever. This should just be a blip for them—Giff's not the type to hold a grudge. But how awkward would it be for them to double-date, to get together at the holidays with their girlfriends if I was one of the girlfriends in question?"

Kresley nodded. "I see your point. But it's kind of a shame. You are one of the steadiest, most dependable people I've ever met, both professionally and personally. For you to do something so—"

"Reckless and self-destructive?"

"I was going to say impetuous. Anyway, for you to

have done that, your feelings for him must be pretty damn strong."

Brooke wanted to deny that she had feelings at all. Instead she settled for a resolute, "I'll get over them."

JAKE RETURNED THE HOSTESS'S smile, trying to project some warmth despite the chilled feeling he hadn't been able to shake this week. This evening in particular, when he should have been at Santa Lucia's, he felt as if he were suffering frostbite from the inside out.

"You're in time for our early-bird dinner specials," she told him, flipping her long hair back off her shoulder. "Right this way and I'll show you to your seat."

"Actually, do you have anything in Maggie's section?"

When the young woman frowned at him, looking puzzled, he tried again. "Megan's?"

"Oh, sure! Meg's one of our most popular waitresses." She lowered her voice to a conspiratorial whisper. "Got a crush?"

"No ma'am, we're just friends," he said. With any luck, allies. Was there a chance that he could win Brooke's sister over to his cause?

He needed all the help he could get. At work, he'd found himself wishing for more calls to distract him— not in the form of tragic accidents, of course, but maybe a few cats stuck in trees. He'd pulled out his cell phone dozens of times, never entirely sure whom he wanted to call more, Giff or Brooke. Talking to Brooke seemed like it might be easier because he at least had a little bit of right on his side. He *knew* deep down that she was just as attracted to him as he was to her; that kiss on Saturday had been spontaneous combustion.

Given the opportunity, maybe he could get through to her, get her to at least consider the idea of dating him.

He suspected that it would be more difficult to face Giff because Jake was so clearly in the wrong. *You don't kiss your best friend's fiancée.* Even if the engagement *had* been a horrible idea. Was Giff missing Brooke as much as he was, sleepless with thoughts of her? Or had Giff resumed business as usual, sorry to see her go but not having a strong emotional reaction to it? Jake would bet his house that it was the latter. But since the two men weren't speaking, Jake had no way of knowing whether his theory panned out.

"Here you go." The hostess indicated a mini-booth for two, and handed him a menu. "The early prices are valid as long as you order before five-thirty. Your server will be with you shortly."

Jake didn't have long to wait before Meg appeared, her bright "welcome to Buck's" smile faltering when she identified him.

"Well, well," she drawled, one hand on her hip. "Look who it is."

He sighed. "I suppose you hate me, too?"

"I try not to hate anyone. It's a karma thing. But, no. I think you hurt my kid sister, for which I'm half tempted to kick your butt. But…"

That one syllable filled him with more hope than he'd experienced all week. "Yeah?"

"But I think in a way, you woke her up some. No of- fense to your buddy, but I think she was sleepwalking when she was dating Giff. She's not happy right now, but I think she has a greater capacity now to be truly happy than she would have if she'd married him."

"Thank you!" He was so grateful to have someone validate his point of view that he could have kissed her. Except he'd already gotten himself in enough trouble that way. "So will you put in a good word for me, help persuade her to talk to me?"

Meg looked sorry for him as she shook her head. "No can do, Romeo. I'm rooting for you two crazy kids, but she's my sister. You made this mess, you're going to have to clean it up alone."

Alone. He almost sneered at the hateful word. Brooke had said once that he came across as a loner and there had been times in the past when he would have agreed. But not after this week, when unfamiliar loneliness had swamped him. He'd lost his best friend and had, for the first time in his life, been on the edge of falling in love, only to lose that, too.

The question now was, how did he get both of those people back?

"I can't believe I'm here." As if seeking divine guidance, Jake cast his eyes heavenward. He hadn't even called first, so there might not be anyone home.

Or maybe he only *hoped* that no one would be home.

Stop being a wuss and go knock on the door. Giff's comment about Grace's birthday being a "family" occasion had been a direct hit. Jake had been bereft this week in part because he'd felt orphaned. When in fact *he* was the one who'd blown off most of his own mother's overtures to come by and have dinner some time, to see for himself the changes in his dad and the McBride household. How could Jake accuse Brooke of emotional cowardice when he wasn't willing to face his own parents?

Besides, Meg's mention of karma had stuck with him. He fervently wanted Giff to forgive him. Maybe Jake should try embracing forgiveness, as well.

Deciding that he just needed to bite the bullet and get this over with, he took the porch stairs two at a time in determined, long-legged strides. It was after eight but, given the long summer days, it wasn't dark out yet. He started to ring the doorbell but it felt silly, too formal considering that he'd grown up in this very house. Instead he rapped on the door, then stood there as ill at ease as a code violator suddenly faced with a surprise fire marshal inspection.

Even from the other side of the door, he could hear his mother's gasp when she saw who it was through the peephole. The door flew open so quickly that he worried about its aged hinges.

"Jake Michael McBride! Oh, is it really you?"

In his memories, his mother was always stooped, looking like a woman with an air of fragility, as if the next hard knock life sent her might be the one that broke her. Other than having the same eyes—eyes he'd inherited—this pink-cheeked woman bore no resemblance to his recollections.

He bent down to hug her. "You look great, Mama."

"This is just so... I can't for the life of me recall the

last time I've had such a surprise!" She suddenly pulled back, her bright gaze turning suspicious. "Wait, there isn't anything wrong, is there? Bad news you felt like you should deliver in person?"

"No." He followed her inside so that they could close the door against any Texas-size mosquitoes that might be lurking about. The furniture in the front den hadn't changed at all, but there were no longer any beer bottles at the foot of his father's recliner, no glasses of whiskey-colored melted ice forming water stains on the hexagonal coffee table. "Not a thing wrong. It was just time."

She swatted at his shoulder, trying for a pseudo-stern expression but too delighted to pull it off. "Well past time, wouldn't you say?"

He ducked his head. "How's Aunt Deb doing after her surgery?"

"Improving nicely." She studied him. "But you didn't drive clear 'cross town to ask me that when you could have picked up a phone. Not that you need an excuse to visit—you're welcome any time, day or night—but what really brings you here, son?"

He got the sense that she already knew. Her tone was so compassionate and encouraging that a lump formed in his throat.

"I thought maybe... I thought I'd come see Dad."

"He's at his Tuesday meeting." She glowed with quiet pride. "He never misses. Jake, he's a different man."

Jake had been skeptical, but after seeing how much his mother had changed for the better, it was impossible to believe that his father hadn't evolved, as well. "I'm glad to hear it."

She squeezed his hand. "You have to promise me you'll stay. He shouldn't be much longer and it would just kill him if he missed you."

"I'll wait," Jake agreed. "I was kind of at loose ends tonight anyway." As soon as he'd said it, he realized how insulting it sounded but Mrs. McBride didn't seem bothered.

"Good, you come into the kitchen and have some of my walnut brownies."

"You made them?" Now that she mentioned it, he could smell them. But he didn't remember her doing much baking during his childhood.

"I did. When you were growing up, it felt like I was working two jobs just to keep you in groceries—I swear I've never seen anyone put away that much food—and of course there was making sure you had rides to and from practice. I didn't have a lot of time..." She trailed off. "I'm sounding like I blame you for my own shortcomings, but that's not how I mean it. Maybe the problem was I didn't *make* time to develop my own hobbies. I do now."

"Good for you." No wonder she looked so much healthier. He couldn't fathom how much easier her life was now that her husband had sobered up and she was no longer responsible for the daily care of a surly adolescent. Regret nipped at him. He'd spent so much time being angry at his parents for his home life that it had never really occurred to him to try to make it better for him and his mom. He could have cooked the occasional dinner for her or thrown in a load of laundry. Instead, he'd escaped whenever he could to the Baker house and his fantasy of belonging to that family instead of his own.

Impulsively he hugged his mother. "You sit down. I'll cut the brownies and pour us some milk."

"Well," his mother breathed. "You are just full of surprises tonight. And you look good, too. So grown!"

Grown, maybe, but not wise. He wished for a moment that he and his mother shared the same easy relationship as Giff and Grace. Giff was always able to ask his mother's advice, but Jake wouldn't even know where to begin.

Which was his own damn fault. If he'd responded to his mother's overtures—even just meeting her for lunch if he was too stubborn to come the house and deal with his father—he could have cultivated a real relationship with her. Then maybe he'd be able to tell her about Brooke without it feeling stilted and unnatural.

"Mom," he said suddenly, "I hope you don't mind, but I plan to be coming by a lot more often."

"If I'd known this was going to be my lucky day, I would have bought a lottery ticket! I think the only way this could get any better is if you met a girl and brought her over some time, too."

He curled his fingers, the image of Brooke's smile washing over him like a ray of sunlight. "Yeah, that would be pretty great. Who knows? Maybe some of your newfound luck will rub off on me."

IT WAS TEN O'CLOCK WHEN Jake insisted on leaving, mostly out of respect to his parents, whose energy seemed to be flagging.

"Sorry," his mother said sheepishly as they walked him to the door, his father displaying none of his old antagonism for the cane he was forced to use. "We're getting old. I'm always asleep before the late-night talk shows start airing."

"You're not old," Jake's father had interrupted firmly, the way he looked at her was mesmerizing. "You're the most beautiful woman in Houston."

She'd giggled—actually *giggled*—as if she were fifteen instead of fifty and then hugged both men at once. "Now, Jake, you promise me that we'll see you again before Fourth of July. I swear I'm not letting go until you do."

"I promise, Mom. And maybe… I'd love to cook dinner for the two of you sometime. You haven't seen my house yet."

His parents exchanged a long glance.

"We thought about it," his mother said. "I wanted to bring you a housewarming gift. But we didn't want to invite ourselves."

He swallowed hard. "Consider yourself officially invited." He returned her hug, then shook his father's hand, amazed by the sheen of tears he saw in his father's eyes.

"I'll walk you to the car," the older McBride said gruffly. There was a ramp on the side of the house that led down to the driveway, so that the man didn't have to use the stairs.

Once they were alone outside, his father began telling him about AA. "You know I was at my meeting tonight? It's not uncommon for people to talk about how they got started drinking…and what finally gave them the impetus to stop. I know you wanted me to quit drinking when you were a boy and I should have. I can't tell you how much I regret hurting you, your mother. Hell, even myself.

"But it wasn't until you moved out that I realized I may have blown my last chance at being a dad to you. Then when you enlisted and left the country, I didn't even know if I'd ever see you again. I had some starts and stops, quitting isn't a one-time decision, it's an ongoing process. But the day I heard you were coming back to Texas, I knew I'd done the right thing. I felt like I was getting a second chance and it's become easier and easier not to miss the booze."

"You sound like you're doing great, Dad. And I'm proud of you."

His father was unabashedly crying now, and Jake was startled to find his own eyes damp.

"I, um, I should get going."

Mr. McBride nodded. "Don't be a stranger."

"I won't." *Not anymore.* He felt as if he'd been given a miracle, suddenly blessed with the warm, bustling mother and proud father he'd always wanted.

Bemused, he drove home, thinking ahead to the fall and wondering for the first time what his holiday schedule would be like. A bachelor with no children and no strong familial ties, he'd always volunteered for extra shifts so that others could spend the time with their loved ones. This year, Jake wanted to be selfish. The only thing that made him grin wider than the idea of trying his hand at a pumpkin pie for his mom was the hope that Brooke might actually be speaking to him again by Thanksgiving.

After tonight, he felt as if anything was possible, buoyed by optimism. And, as he pulled into his driveway, it seemed as if the universe was already responding to his positive thinking.

"I'll be damned."

Giff's car was parked near the house, and Giff himself was sprawled back across the hood, looking up at the stars. He didn't look as if he were lying in wait for a second round of hand-to-hand combat.

Hoping for the best, Jake hopped out of his car.

"Great view you have out here," Giff called. "I'd forgotten the night sky could look like that."

"How long have you been out here?" Jake asked.

"About fifteen minutes. Mom made me bring you a piece of cake. It's in the car if you want it."

So Grace had guilted her son into coming? It wasn't as encouraging as Giff having the idea all on his own, but it was a start. "Actually, I'm stuffed. Mom filled me up with walnut brownies."

Giff propped himself up on his elbows. "You saw your mother? No kidding?"

"Dad, too. They look fantastic."

Giff let out a low whistle. "Didn't think I'd see the day. Mom said we just had to be patient, but then, she always chooses to believe the best about you. Me, I didn't think you'd get your head out of your butt."

Jake was shocked, not at the cynical way Giff was talking to him—he was obviously still angry—but because his friend had never really expressed an opinion on whether Jake spent time with his folks or not. He'd certainly never been critical about it before.

"I thought you understood why I wasn't nostalgic for home. Just from the few times you visited when we were kids, you saw what it was like."

"Yeah. When we were kids. I got it. But your mom's been telling you that he's cleaned up his act, and it galled me that you wouldn't at least give him a chance. Do you know what I'd give for one more day with my father? To get his opinion on my life or just hang out and watch the Cotton Bowl? You had an opportunity I would have mortgaged my soul for and never cared enough to take it. I've resented the hell out of you for it."

Jake was stunned. Gifford Baker was jealous of him?

Giff swung himself off the front of the car. "I realized a long time ago that my father would never know my children. And after Mom got sick, I started to worry that neither would she. When I met Brooke, she seemed so perfect, so right for me, that I got carried away. I went from wondering if I was falling in love to imagining Mom's face on my wedding day and how happy she'd be holding a grandbaby. I may have skipped a couple of steps."

"But that doesn't excuse what I did," Jake said.

"No. It doesn't. But it was my mother's venerable opinion over dinner that now *I* am the one with his head up his posterior. I've already lost a dad and risked losing a mother, so what kind of idiot would it make me to willingly sacrifice the closest thing I've ever had to a brother?"

Jake's relief was too poignant, too big, to squeeze into words. He nodded his head repeatedly, not sure exactly what he was agreeing with but hoping Giff wouldn't think it was the "idiot" part. Finally he croaked, "Thank you."

"I saw her yesterday. Brooke. She brought back some stuff she had of mine, including the ring. And I felt bad for her. The poor girl looks like she's having a rough time. But that was it, some friendly pity and 'oh, so that's where my sunglasses have been.' If I'd loved her enough to marry her, there should have been a lot more, shouldn't there? Rage, hurt, some kind of second-guessing myself on whether to fight for her."

Wanting to tread carefully here, Jake simply said, "I guess so."

Giff shoved his hands into his pockets and stared him down. "I guess the big question now is, do you care enough to fight for her?"

"Um, you mean fight *you?*"

"No, dumbass." Giff surprised him by laughing. "What I mean is the Midsummer Night Gala this Saturday. It's to raise money to fight childhood leukemia. Brooke will be covering it as part of her lifestyles and society beat. And I just happen to have a ticket it turns out I won't be using."

Jake felt poleaxed. "You would do that for me?"

"I'm just giving you the ticket, man. You sink or swim on your own. And if it's the former, I reserve the right to take vengeful glee in your downfall."

"Deal."

Chapter Sixteen

"Kresley, I feel like a moron!" Brooke fidgeted on the padded antique bench, keeping her voice down so that she didn't offend any society matrons. "A glittery, be-winged moron. *Why* did you tell Sugar I agreed to come in costume?"

Sugar Reese-Archibald, daughter of one millionaire and wife of another, was the brains behind tonight's fund-raiser.

"It's a *costume* ball. And she didn't so much ask as decreed."

It had worked, to a point. Most women were in costume, but the majority of men had chosen black-tie instead.

"Go mingle," Kresley advised. "There are worse things than spending the evening in a posh ballroom, surrounded by rich men and champagne fountains."

"Yeah? I didn't see you jumping at this opportunity." She knew she was bordering on churlish, but she was having trouble getting in the party-going spirit—the latest on a list of difficulties this week. She was also having trouble sleeping, eating and going for more than sixty seconds without thinking about Jake.

Shoot. She'd made it all the way to fifty-five that time.

"*I* am heavily pregnant," Kresley reminded her. "No one wants to see this body in a pair of sparkly tights and a fairy dress. Besides, the guests there are already comfortable with you. So many of them know you through society weddings or, well…"

Giff. A lot of the people who could afford to come to this event were associates of his. They'd originally planned to attend as a couple. He'd mentioned when she gave him the ring that he wasn't planning to come after all.

"I don't consider my ticket a waste of money, since it's for such a worthy cause," he'd said, "but I've been invited to something else that night."

She suspected that the real reason for his change of plans was kindness to her. He'd known she'd be here for the paper and hadn't wanted to make her evening more awkward. He'd been so gracious when she gave him the ring back that she'd faltered, asking herself again how she could let go of such a flawless guy. *Because you're fixated on another man entirely.* Even if she stayed strong and never contacted Jake, it wouldn't be fair for her to date someone else right now, much less marry.

"All right," Brooke resolved. "I am going now. And I will be festive and witty."

"You make me proud. Speaking of which, the article we ran on Jake was fantastic. I've already had people e-mail me."

That certainly put tonight in perspective. The remainder of the evening couldn't be anywhere near as painful as writing that had been. She'd been doing a lot of writing lately, not just for work, and found it cathartic. But that particular piece had felt as if she were gouging out her own heart with a pen.

After saying goodbye, Brooke stood and checked her make-up in a huge oval mirror. Her eyes and lips were dusted in the same shimmery lavender, and she'd let Meg talk her into sprinkling body glitter across her face, neck and exposed arms. The dress she'd chosen for tonight was fairly simple—a white, off-the-shoulder, bubble gown shot through with silver threads. But the garland of flowers that kept slipping down on her head, to say nothing of the darned wings, were working her last nerve.

As she returned to the ballroom, a story began to spin in her head of its own volition, about an extremely cranky fairy with poison-tipped wings. It made her laugh, drawing questioning glances from the masked waiter who passed by with a tray of duck pâté appetizers. From another waiter, she accepted a flute of champagne and had just taken her first sip when someone tapped her shoulder.

Since Sugar had been introducing her to people all night—Important Benefactors who wanted to make sure their names were mentioned in the paper—Brooke expected to once again find tonight's reigning Queen Titania with some local celebrity or business mogul in tow.

"Jake!" It was all she could do to keep from dropping her champagne. "What are you doing here?"

"Looking for you," he said simply. His gaze dropped to her sandaled feet, then slowly traveled back up. His grin was a mile wide. "And I am *so* glad I found you."

This was worse than those nightmares in which she couldn't find the classroom where her exam was, only to realize she was standing naked in the school hallways. No woman should have to run into a man from her romantic past *while wearing wings*.

She eyed his black tuxedo pointedly. "It's a shame no one told you it was a themed costume ball. You could have come as Bottom. He's the one who turns into an ass," she said sweetly.

He pursed his lips. "Yes, I believe we've already discussed my familiarity with Shakespeare."

His reminding her of that conversation also reminded her of how unexpectedly close she'd felt to him during their trip to Tennessee. How different would those few days have been if they hadn't also been marred by her guilt over Giff? *Who is no longer in the picture.* The realization both exhilarated and frightened her. He'd been not only an obstacle between her and Jake but a buffer, a guarantee—she'd thought—that she wouldn't develop any imprudent feelings for the breathtaking firefighter.

He really was painfully handsome; looking at him was reminiscent of staring into the sun. But she couldn't look away. Her gaze was riveted to his face as if she had to memorize everything about him, in case they were separated again. She'd missed him so much. Although she'd insisted to Meg and Kresley that most of her unhappiness came from guilt and the hassle of calling off the wedding, with Jake now standing in front of her, she couldn't deny the truth.

"I told you I didn't want to see you," she said hesitantly. Would it make her look weak if she implored him to forget she ever said that?

"I know." His voice was strained. "I was hoping I could change your mind. And that…you might dance with me?"

"Okay." Dancing gave her a socially acceptable excuse to remain close to him without the pesky requirement of making coherent conversation. There were so many things she could say, but none seemed right.

With her hand in his, the Midsummer Night Gala really did take on a magical, otherworldly quality. She couldn't believe she was in Jake's arms again, free to enjoy it this time without conflicted feelings. He held her far closer than he should, and she luxuriated in the muscular contours beneath the civilized jacket and tie.

"How did you know I would be here?" she murmured softly, as if their regular speaking voices might break the spell.

"Sorry I found you?"

"No." Even the damn fairy wings were worth it if she got this in return. "Just curious."

"Giff told me."

She lost her rhythm and would have tripped, but Jake held on to her. "Giff? Gifford Baker?" Not that she knew of another one, but still.

"He's obviously a better man than I am, because if I lost you… Not that I have you to lose," he admitted. But he wanted her. That was crystal clear in his steady, unapologetic gaze. "I have something to ask you, Brooke."

"Y-yes?"

"Will you have dinner with me next week? Not because you were assigned a story or because you were ambushed or as a favor to anyone." He sounded boyishly vulnerable, yet incredibly sexy. "But just because you want to be with me?"

When had they stopped moving? "I do," Brooke said. She nibbled her bottom lip, her pulse frantic as she willed him closer. "I want that very much."

His mouth brushed over hers, no more than a whisper of contact. Then he found the shell of her ear, making her shiver in his arms. "Do you want to get out of here?"

Anywhere they could be alone sounded like paradise to her. "God, yes."

His eyes glittered with desire. "I was hoping you'd say that."

OUTSIDE OF THE BALLROOM, in a dimly lit, plushly carpeted corridor, Jake was unable to resist the impulse to kiss her any longer. *Really* kiss her, the kind of kiss that involved the entire body and no holding back. They were both nearly panting when they stopped to catch their breath.

"What now?" she asked, moaning softly when he ran his lips down the side of her neck. "Your place, mine? Whose car do we take? Right now, I can't even remember where I'm parked."

"We could just check into a room here." He was

stunned by his own boldness. It was too soon, too risky. What if she was offended by the suggestion?

But her eyes had heated to molten sapphire, and it only took her a second to respond with a husky "Perfect."

The few minutes spent at the lobby counter passed in a dazed blur as he tried unsuccessfully to comprehend his good fortune. Before Jake knew it, he and Brooke were in a darkened room, looking out at the glittery view below, and he still couldn't fathom how—or even when—he'd talked her into forgiving him.

"You're not mad anymore?" he pressed. "That I kissed you?"

She grabbed the lapels of his jacket. "Actually, I was hoping you'd kiss me some more."

He cupped his hand behind her nape. "Anything you want."

"Anything?" she purred. "Do you think you could help me out of my...wings?"

Chuckling, he obliged, also taking the time to shove off his own jacket. Pieces of clothing hit the floor between kisses, and he found himself gifted with an unexpected image that would be forever seared onto his memory: Brooke wearing only a pair of sparkly high heels, a lopsided flower garland and a naughty smile.

He pressed her to the bed with the newly formed goal of kissing every creamy inch of her. "I don't deserve you," he murmured above the flat dip of her navel.

Brooke would have told him he was wrong, but she couldn't speak. His mouth was making her crazy. She had no words or coherent thoughts. She had no inhibitions. She had no plan. She had no filter. She was bared to him in every way possible. The sensations Jake had ignited beneath her skin overwhelmed her, surging up and hurtling her into a shattering release.

She cried out, unnerved by the sheer intensity of what she'd experienced, but then he was kissing her, and the craving that should have been sated built again. Murmuring her name, he slid inside her, not trying to slow her down when she set a savage, frantic rhythm that sent them both over the edge.

Brooke felt flung from her body. Dots swam in front of her eyes. Her lungs would never have enough oxygen in them again.

"I love you."

She was actually so dazed from the unprecedented, soul-shaking sex that it took her a moment to realize she'd said the words. It was like watching a dubbed movie where the characters' dialogue was a fraction of a second ahead of their mouth.

"Oh, God." She twisted away from him. *Have you lost your mind?* "I shouldn't have said that."

Jake seemed untroubled by her impulsive pillow talk. On the contrary, his smile was bright enough to light up all of Harris County. "I love you, too."

"No. No, no, that's—" She scrambled toward the edge of the bed, taking as much of the sheet with her as possible. "I was momentarily confused by the mind-blowing sex. I don't… That wasn't me."

"The hell it wasn't," he said lightly, his smile not dimming. "I was there. I know."

"We got carried away." Panic was rising within her—all the emotions she'd tried to repress in the name of order suddenly spewing forth. She'd been beyond "carried away"; she had been completely without rational thought. She'd ended her engagement less than a week ago, and now she was falling into bed with another man and telling him she *loved* him?

It was the nightmare version of herself, the one she'd always feared she might wake up and see in the mirror, the passion-driven dreamer who would make Meg and Didi look like calm analysts in comparison.

Taking deep breaths, she tried to find that inner calm. "Jake, I do care about you—"

"It's more than that." He tugged on a lock of her hair. "Don't downplay it and try to make it less than it is."

"Don't rush me! I've only known you a little over a month."

He quirked an eyebrow but spared her the embarrassment of pointing out that she'd gotten *engaged* after only two months.

Then he just shook his head, smiling. "I'm too relaxed to fight. Come to bed, and we'll sort this out in the morning."

She doubted she could be so close to him for that long without jumping him again. He was a detriment to her willpower. And her ability to think. And to the person she'd tried so hard to be.

"Jake," she said carefully, "I need time to process. And it's better if we don't make love again. For a while anyway."

His jaw dropped. "I don't believe this. We were *phenomenal* together."

"This isn't a rejection," she tried to reassure him.

Considering that she'd just stepped back into her dress and was casting about the room to find her shoes, he might not believe her. "I just need to—"

"Squish your feelings down inside some box? To have inhuman control over yourself? I want to be with you, Brooke. But I want to *be* together, freely and honestly. A relationship with me would not be as cordial and antiseptic as the one you had with...as the one you had before. It would be messy and real and imperfect and deliriously good."

She believed him. He did tend to make her feel delirious.

"I'm not sure I'm ready for that," she admitted. "You make it sound good—or feel good, at the very least—but I never wanted all that passion and crisis."

"Then you don't want me?" he asked, that hint of vulnerability back in his voice.

And I put it there. She wasn't sure she wanted to be responsible for someone else's emotional well-being, wasn't sure she could ever be comfortable with someone having that much power over her. "You know that's not true. I just want to slow down, think it over."

"Okay." He looked away from her. "But it seems to me like you're always finding excuses. You're too busy thinking about your life or chronicling other people's lives or planning out the life you think you want to actually *live* your life. If you're not careful, Brooke, it's going to pass you by."

BROOKE TRIED TO TREAT HERSELF on Sunday, sleeping in late and fixing herself fresh waffles with strawberries and powdered sugar. But nothing she did alone was going to be as rewarding as what she and Jake had shared last night. Besides, she couldn't dredge up enough of an appetite to enjoy the waffles.

Last night had been such a roller coaster of emotional highs and lows. Jake made her feel far too much. Too uncertain about herself and her goals, too angry, too scared, too turned on. It was disconcerting.

But did that mean she was willing to give him up, especially now that Giff had implied they had his blessing? She was free to follow where her heart might lead. If only she were brave enough to give up her death grip on the compass, the map and the GPS.

When her phone rang, she jumped. Could it be Jake? Whatever else she had yet to decide, there was no question that she wanted to hear his voice.

But it was Kresley. "Are you watching the local news?"

"No, why?" Brooke reached for her remote.

"I don't suppose you know if Jake's working today?"

Brooke's breath caught as her television flickered to life and orange flames filled the screen. A reporter's voice-over was explaining that a fire had started in the early-morning hours in one of the units of the Mesquite Bend Apartments, a much older complex than the one where Brooke lived. Because of the lack of rain this year, the woods behind Mesquite Bend had quickly ignited, too.

Action shots showed firefighters in uniform battling the blaze with water and other materials. It was impossible to tell beneath the many pounds of gear who any of them were.

"He should be off duty," she heard herself say. "He might have been scheduled to go in later, but he wasn't working this morning."

He'd wanted to wake up with her this morning, in that hotel bed where she'd had the best sex of her life. If she'd stayed, she might *know* at this exact moment that he was safe instead of staring at her TV and merely praying that he was.

"Do you think they called in extra help?" Kresley asked cautiously. "It looks like they could use it."

True. And he was trained for this. Was it selfish that she was hoping he was miles away from the scene, instead of hoping that he was on site saving as many lives as possible? Jake challenged her to be brave, but he didn't seem to realize how much he was asking.

Any relationship carried with it risk of being hurt. But to fall for a guy who did *this* for a living? It was like painting a large bull's-eye right over her heart.

"Do we have someone covering the scene?" Brooke asked.

"Yeah, Whalen's down there."

"I want to go meet up with him." Even if Jake wasn't there, she felt compelled to take a closer look at what it was he did, who he was.

"Are you sure that's a good idea?" Kresley asked gently. "It's not like you'll be able to help. They've got the crowd roped off. And the last thing you want is to distract him if he is there!"

"I won't," Brooke promised. "You know me. I'm not

going to cause some big scene, I just want to stand back and watch. It will make me feel closer to him."

"Okay. Call my cell if you learn anything more."

"Same here."

Brooke was still blocks away from the apartment complex when smoke began to tickle the back of her throat and her eyes burned. A black plume was snaking toward the sky, so sinister-looking that Brooke could swear it was a living thing, bent on malevolence. Even though, rationally, she could tell that the fire was smaller than it had been during the newscast she'd seen, it was far scarier in person than on her television.

Whalen was waiting for her at the perimeter of the crowd. "Kresley said you were on your way. They think some faulty wiring may have caused this, but aren't sure. The fire chief said it's now classified as under control."

She stared openmouthed at the inferno that had once been people's homes. "*That's* under control?"

"Well, it's not spreading anymore. It's still going to take a lot of work to put out, but they seem to have it contained."

Generations of evolutionary instinct were prompting her to get as far from here as possible. "Can we get closer?"

Announcing that they were with the press, Whalen shouldered a path through the gathered witnesses, some of whom had no doubt lived here. Even from a comparatively safe distance, Brooke could feel the brutal heat against her skin. She squinted against the smoke on the wind.

"Oh, God, I think I know him." She couldn't be one-hundred percent sure but she thought that the young guy who'd just removed his helmet and was talking to a city official was Ben Hoskins, the cute young fireman who'd flirted with her when she came to visit—

"Brooke?" It wasn't Hoskins who noticed her behind the tape, but Jake, who was also on her side of the safety line.

Thank you, God. "You're okay!" She wanted to run to him, but settled for muttering apologies and "excuse me" as she threaded her way past other people and reached his side. There, she threw her arms around him and covered his face in kisses. "Oh, Lord, I'm glad to see you. I saw this on the news and I—"

"I'm fine," he promised her, cupping her cheeks and kissing her squarely on the mouth. "But you shouldn't sprint to the fire scene every time one breaks out. I wouldn't be able to work effectively, worrying about you."

"But you're not working now?"

"I came by on my way home to see if they needed help. I have to get my gear, but then I'll come back. It's going to take a while to put this down for good. Why don't you go home, and I'll call you tonight?"

She didn't want to be at her place, cooped up and scared for his safety. Knowing it was a bizarre request but hoping he wouldn't mind, she asked, "Could I wait at the fire station?"

He regarded her thoughtfully. "I have a compromise. What if you waited at my place? Unless you think that's too weird. I know you've never even seen my house before, but—"

"Thank you," she said gratefully as they made their way back to where they'd each had to park on the opposite side of the road. "I can't explain why being there will make me feel better about your safety, but it will."

He gave her a key, quick directions and a laughing admonishment not to rifle through his nightstand unless she was prepared to be shocked. She knew he was only making absurd jokes to try to take her mind off of being scared for him. It didn't work, but she wished it had. She was sick and tired of being scared.

JAKE WASN'T REALLY SURE what to expect when he walked through his front door. He'd been shocked to find Brooke at the scene of the fire this morning and even more surprised that she'd preferred to wait here instead of in the comfort of her own place. Last night she'd practically fled after they'd made love. Maybe he'd judged her too harshly and she really had needed just some time alone to think over everything. But he couldn't help wondering, would she have tracked him down on her own like this without the fire? He didn't want her showing up in his life voluntarily only when she was concerned about him.

"Hello?"

"In the kitchen," she called back.

His house was so small, it was a matter of feet to cut through the living room into the kitchen. Brooke was scowling into the open pantry, a copper teapot was burbling on the stove and several pieces of legal paper were crumpled into yellow balls atop his yard-sale-find table. And just like that, his chest swelled with the absolute contented peace of *home*. Hell, if concern was what it took to have Brooke come to him, he could work with that. He fought fires for a living, didn't he?

As she turned in his direction, pure happiness to see him washed away her frown. "I'm so glad you're okay. And thank you for calling me from the station."

"I didn't want you to worry."

She gestured toward the pantry. "I had this grand idea about making you dinner after a rough day, but I'm missing at least two key ingredients for every recipe I've come up with so far."

"I'd settle for a hug after a rough day," he suggested.

Immediately the contents of his pantry were forgotten. "I didn't know big, strong guys needed hugs," she told him, folding into his embrace.

"We do when it means getting closer to a beautiful woman."

She tipped her face up and kissed him so sweetly that Jake found himself yearning for a future of this— walking through a door and knowing that this, that *she*, awaited him on the other side. Their kiss graduated from tender to playful to outright sexy and just as he was considering carrying her to the couch in the next room, she pulled away.

"You've got to be tired after today," she said shyly.

Not *that* tired.

"Want to sit down? I was making tea. I could pour you a cup."

"Sure." Maybe their disconnects so far hadn't been *all* about her running away; maybe he needed to stop coming on so strong. If fussing over him and taking a minute helped her feel more comfortable with their relationship—nothing in the world would convince him that this was only lust, not after the wealth of relief he'd seen in her eyes today—then why deny her? He could keep from pouncing on her long enough to let *her* come to *him*. Probably.

"So what's all this?" he asked, glancing from what looked like a dog-eared legal pad, full of writing, to the wadded up pages that apparently hadn't made the cut.

"I hope you don't mind. I didn't have my laptop with me and saw the pad by the phone. I could buy you a new one."

He laughed. "Can't we just work out some kind of trade?"

"Maybe." She blushed as she said it, but her eyes sparkled mischievously. "Anyway, I just had some ideas I wanted to write down before I forgot them, and then I got caught up in it. Helped me pass the time."

He reached for the pad. "So can I read it?"

"No!" She cleared her throat. "I mean, some day, when it's actually in some sort of articulate form, yes. Right now it's a hodgepodge of shorthand notes and ideas. I like my job at the paper. I know that most of the wedding write-ups I do aren't Pulitzer material, but there's a lot to enjoy, including great coworkers and the occasional opportunity to cover a story that's special. Like the one on you."

Now *he* felt like blushing. He knew people were

reading it, because several people had mentioned it to him, seeming genuinely interested in his travels and asking questions about places he would recommend and places he would want to visit again after he'd seen all fifty states. "Thank you."

She set a cup down in front of him, then took the seat next to him, curling her legs beneath her and looking more like an eager high school senior on career day than a thirty-year-old woman. "So I don't want to quit, but I've been thinking…. I can keep my job and try other things, right? Nothing's stopping me from writing in my spare time. I might get rejections, but the day job will keep paying my bills. And also pay for the occasional medicinal margarita."

He laughed. "I think that sounds like a great idea."

"I was hoping you would say that because you remember how we talked about that travel writing?" When he nodded, she asked, "How would you feel about letting me tag along on your trip to Hawaii?"

Jake was too startled to respond. What happened to her needing time and space?

"I wouldn't be writing about you this time," she clarified nervously. "And I certainly wouldn't expect a free ride. I—"

"Brooke. I am okay. I was not in mortal danger today, I wasn't even injured. You don't have to cross an ocean with me just because you're relieved."

Her bottom lip trembled. "I was being too pushy, huh?"

"That's not it. Push as much you want. I guess, the important part is make sure *you* want it. Last night, for instance, I thought we were on the same page—until you ran out the door so fast you left a trail of smoke behind."

"I'm sorry about that," she said. "I don't have much experience in that area, certainly none like that, and I wasn't sure how to act. I definitely hadn't planned to say I love you, and there didn't seem like a graceful way to take it back. But I did a lot of thinking today."

"Because of the fire?" he asked.

She shrugged. "Yeah, maybe, but just because sometimes it takes an outside event to trigger an epiphany doesn't make the epiphany less true. When I was driving to the Mesquite Bend apartments, I was obviously really worried for you, but I also realized I was really glad that I'd blurted out my real feelings for you last night. If you *had* been hurt today…" She shuddered when she said it, and he reached across the table to squeeze her hand comfortingly.

Taking a deep breath, she tried again. "Life is uncertain. You told me once that anyone who tries to act otherwise is either in denial or a coward."

He flinched, hearing his words repeated like that. It made his opinion of her sound far too harsh. "Brooke—"

"No, you were right. I'm not saying we should all give up and just live in anarchy," she stipulated, "but I have to accept that my feelings are not always going to be predictable and regimented and that not all my relationships are going to follow terms and conditions I dreamed up when I was twelve because I thought it would keep me safer."

"You really were a very goal-oriented child."

She laughed. "Anyway, things happen to people, even people who don't fight fires for a living. And I don't want to think that if I'm hit by a meteor tomorrow that I'll leave behind people who never really knew how I felt because I was too scared to let myself express it. To let myself feel it in the first place. I do love you. It sounds insane when I hear it out loud—we're pretty different, aren't we?—but I think I've tried to be sane too hard for too long."

I am the luckiest SOB on the face of the earth. Pure joy expanded inside him, making his chest tight. "I think I can help with that."

She slid out of her chair, and he pulled her into his lap. "I love you, too," he said. "But we can take it slow if this starts to freak you out."

"I'm not so worried about that anymore," she told him as she raised her face to his. "You make me brave."

And you make me happier than I ever thought possible. He didn't say the words aloud now, too busy kissing her, but he'd tell her later. And often.

Epilogue

The high-pitched squeals coming through the cell phone were so loud that Brooke held it away from her ear.

Jake, who was on the balcony proofreading a humorous piece she'd drafted about honeymoons, winced in sympathy.

"You eloped?" Meg demanded at an ear-splitting decibel. *"You?"*

"Some moms pass on their wedding dress to their daughters, I guess our mother just passed on this quaint tradition." She grinned. "It was *very* passionate and romantic."

This got a thumbs-up from Brooke's husband of the past forty-eight hours. They really should have started calling their loved ones yesterday with the news, but they'd been...otherwise occupied. His parents—two charming people she'd come to adore—had not been surprised by the announcement and had welcomed her warmly to the family.

"We'll have a huge party to celebrate when we get back," Brooke said. "Wanna help with that?"

Meg, whose latest venture was a party-planning

business, laughed in delight. "If it turns out well, you have to let me use you as a testimonial. And now that your last name's McBride, people won't even know we're related."

Brooke McBride. She grinned stupidly, thrilled with her new name. During the past six weeks of dating Jake, she'd decided without a doubt that she wanted to spend the rest of her life with him, but she'd been having trouble getting excited about looking for another dress and sending out invitations. Again. And even though Giff was being a veritable saint about their relationship, neither she nor Jake could imagine asking *him* to be the best man at *their* wedding. It seemed unbelievably tacky.

So when Jake had half-jokingly pointed out that they could elope during their trip to the islands, Brooke had decided it was perfect, in an ironic, fate-getting-the-last-laugh kind of way.

"Do you have pictures? Did you tell Mom and Dad yet?"

"Yes and yes. I'll give you all the details when I get home," Brooke promised. "But we've got other calls to make." Eventually.

"All right. Give your gorgeous new hubby a hug from me!"

"Will do." Brooke hung up and went to join Jake in the tropical breeze, bracing an arm on either side of his chair. "In case I haven't told you in the last five minutes, I love you."

"Back at you." He kissed her deeply, then rose, scooping her up and carrying her toward the bed.

Brooke giggled. "You do realize you have over twenty states left to go. You may have set the bar too high—it'll be impossible to top this trip."

Waggling his eyebrows at her, he said, "I have some ideas. Wanna hear about them?"

She shook her head. "Surprise me."

* * * * *

Giff may not have found the right bride...yet!
You'll be happy to hear he's got his own
happily-ever-after story in
TEXAS BABY
coming this September
only from Harlequin American Romance!

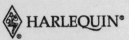

HARLEQUIN®

COMING NEXT MONTH

Available July 13, 2010

#1313 THE LAWMAN'S LITTLE SURPRISE
Babies & Bachelors USA
Roxann Delaney

#1314 DEXTER: HONORABLE COWBOY
The Codys: The First Family of Rodeo
Marin Thomas

#1315 A MOM FOR CALLIE
Laura Bradford

#1316 FIREFIGHTER DADDY
Fatherhood
Lee McKenzie

REQUEST YOUR FREE BOOKS!
2 FREE NOVELS PLUS 2 FREE GIFTS!

HARLEQUIN®

American ★ Romance®

Love, Home & Happiness!

YES! Please send me 2 FREE Harlequin® American Romance® novels and my 2 FREE gifts (gifts are worth about $10). After receiving them, if I don't wish to receive any more books, I can return the shipping statement marked "cancel." If I don't cancel, I will receive 4 brand-new novels every month and be billed just $4.24 per book in the U.S. or $4.99 per book in Canada. That's a saving of at least 15% off the cover price! It's quite a bargain! Shipping and handling is just 50¢ per book.* I understand that accepting the 2 free books and gifts places me under no obligation to buy anything. I can always return a shipment and cancel at any time. Even if I never buy another book from Harlequin, the two free books and gifts are mine to keep forever.

154/354 HDN E5LG

Name	(PLEASE PRINT)

Address	Apt. #

City	State/Prov.	Zip/Postal Code

Signature (if under 18, a parent or guardian must sign)

Mail to the **Harlequin Reader Service:**
IN U.S.A.: P.O. Box 1867, Buffalo, NY 14240-1867
IN CANADA: P.O. Box 609, Fort Erie, Ontario L2A 5X3

Not valid for current subscribers to Harlequin® American Romance® books.

Want to try two free books from another line?
Call 1-800-873-8635 or visit www.morefreebooks.com.

* Terms and prices subject to change without notice. Prices do not include applicable taxes. N.Y. residents add applicable sales tax. Canadian residents will be charged applicable provincial taxes and GST. Offer not valid in Quebec. This offer is limited to one order per household. All orders subject to approval. Credit or debit balances in a customer's account(s) may be offset by any other outstanding balance owed by or to the customer. Please allow 4 to 6 weeks for delivery. Offer available while quantities last.

Your Privacy: Harlequin is committed to protecting your privacy. Our Privacy Policy is available online at www.eHarlequin.com or upon request from the Reader Service. From time to time we make our lists of customers available to reputable third parties who may have a product or service of interest to you. If you would prefer we not share your name and address, please check here. ☐

Help us get it right—We strive for accurate, respectful and relevant communications. To clarify or modify your communication preferences, visit us at www.ReaderService.com/consumerschoice.

HAR10R

HARLEQUIN®

A *Romance*

FOR EVERY MOOD™

Spotlight on
Heart & Home

Heartwarming romances
where love can happen
right when you least expect it.

See the next page to enjoy a sneak peek
from Silhouette Special Edition®,
a Heart and Home series.

*Introducing McFARLANE'S PERFECT BRIDE
by USA TODAY bestselling author Christine Rimmer,
from Silhouette Special Edition®.*

Entranced. Captivated. Enchanted.

Connor sat across the table from Tori Jones and couldn't help thinking that those words exactly described what effect the small-town schoolteacher had on him. He might as well stop trying to tell himself he wasn't interested. He was powerfully drawn to her.

Clearly, he should have dated more when he was younger.

There had been a couple of other women since Jennifer had walked out on him. But he had never been entranced. Or captivated. Or enchanted.

Until now.

He wanted her—*her,* Tori Jones, in particular. Not just someone suitably attractive and well-bred, as Jennifer had been. Not just someone sophisticated, sexually exciting and discreet, which pretty much described the two women he'd dated after his marriage crashed and burned.

It came to him that he…he *liked* this woman. And that was new to him. He liked her quick wit, her wisdom and her big heart. He liked the passion in her voice when she talked about things she believed in.

He liked *her.* And suddenly it mattered all out of proportion that she might like him, too.

Was he losing it? He couldn't help but wonder. Was he cracking under the strain—of the soured economy, the McFarlane House setbacks, his divorce, the scary changes in his son? Of the changes he'd decided he needed to make in his life and himself?

Strangely, right then, on his first date with Tori Jones, he didn't care if he just might be going over the edge. He was having a great time—having *fun*, of all things—and he didn't want it to end.

Is Connor finally able to admit his feelings to Tori, and are they reciprocated?
Find out in MCFARLANE'S PERFECT BRIDE
by USA TODAY bestselling author Christine Rimmer.
Available July 2010,
only from Silhouette Special Edition®.

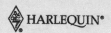